WRITERS REPUBLIC

WHAT IS MEANT...

Will Be

THE LIFE & TIMES OF SHAWNE THOMAS VOL 3

TRE KEAHEY

WRITERS REPUBLIC L.L.C.
515 Summit Ave. Unit R1
Union City, NJ 07087, USA

Website: *www.writersrepublic.com*
Hotline: *1-877-656-6838*
Email: *info@writersrepublic.com*

Ordering Information:
Quantity sales. Special discounts are available on quantity purchases by corporations, associations, and others. For details, contact the publisher at the address above.

Library of Congress Control Number:	2023901272	
ISBN-13:	979-8-88810-430-9	[Paperback Edition]
	979-8-88810-431-6	[Hardback Edition]
	979-8-88810-432-3	[Digital Edition]

Rev. date: 01/30/2023

The Recap

Shawne's control over his life is slowly slipping away from him. He went from having all he could dream of, his wife, child, beautiful homes. A career and championship in the sport he grew up loving... To an addictive love triangle with a baby on the way, and a possible connection to murder investigation. Shawne tries to keep a step ahead and play it smoothly, until the events of September 11th, 2001 changes him, possibly forever.

Chapter 1

The Aftermath

After several hours of searching through the damage, a police officer saw a light, blinking rapidly.

"Aye! I may have something over here!" The officer yelled.

A strobing flashlight was on, and first responders quickly zeroed in and began pulling, lifting and cutting away the wreckage.

Meanwhile in Denver, still hysterical, Shawne is unable to do anything to help. He can't fly out anywhere, they were unable to rent a vehicle, and he can't reach Tasha by phone. He and Ro went back upstairs to the room. Shawne is sitting on the edge of the chair, clutching the sides of his head, rocking and shaking.

"Bro, you gotta calm down and trust that she got out." Roman said to Shawne, trying to console him.

"I should have just did it, Ro. She wanted me to tell Jaz about her and the baby, and everything would've been all good between us. But I kept puttin' it off. Tryin' to walk safely down the middle. Ro what if she didn't get out, Man?" Shawne shouted, jumping up.

Roman grabbed a hold of his weeping friend. He hugged him tightly, and began to pray aloud. "Father God, we come before You right now hurting, yet humbled, knowing that everything that happens, is done to glorify Your holy name. Lord, bring peace to us Father, to Shawne, our families and friends. Place Your mighty loving Arms around Tasha and that sweet baby boy growing inside her. Protect them from harm, Lord. We don't know why this horrific act was carried out, but we know Your Will be done. Soothe my brother's heart. Open it, and pour Your love into him. I ask of these blessings in the loving name of Your Son, Jesus Christ, with thanksgiving… Amen." Roman let Shawne go.

"Amen." Shawne muttered, taking a deep breath and closing his eyes.

"Trust His power Cali. Try callin' Miss Linda from the hotel phone. You only been

callin' cell phones right?"

"Yeah, good thinkin'." Shawne replied, picking up the phone to dial Tasha's mother.

"Hello?" She answered.

"Ma? You okay?"

"Shawne. Baby no, I'm a nervous wreck. I spoke to her earlier this morning and haven't heard from her since." Ms. Keyes stated.

"Mommy." Shawne started, looked at Roman, then continued. "God… is in control."

Ms. Keyes began to softly sob. "Shawne, knowing what you went through with your family, to hear you profess that, brings me comfort Son."

Roman whispered that he was going to his room to try and call Erica. Shawne continued talking with Ms. Keyes.

In Los Angeles, Aunt Sheryl and Tiffany are still watching the news unfold in New York City. "Mama, you ok?" Tiffany asked her mother.

Aunt Sheryl is still in shock from the news she received from Roman. "Tiff, what I'm about to tell you goes no further than this room. This ain't your issue to fix or settle. You got it?" Sheryl sternly warned.

"Yeah Mama. What is it?"

"Shawne has a baby on the way. And not with Jazmin."

"This whole time he been lyin' to us! All of us!"

"Tiffany. It's between him and Jazmin. He told me…"

"He told you, but not me?" Tiffany interrupted.

"He told me bits and pieces. His friend just told me about the baby. He didn't tell you because he knew how you would react."

"Imma wait 'til he tells us. Then I'll show his ass how Imma trip out."

"No. When he tells us, we're gonna support him as best as possible. He's going through enough right now and it's only gonna get worse when Jaz finds out."

Jazmin and Crystal are in the office watching television news coverage and talking.

"Should I feel bad knowing that Shawne's mistress is possibly… You know."

"Dead. I know you can't stand her, but you don't wish her dead J."

"I'm not, but I don't think my marriage will ever work as long as she is.. You know."

"Alive. She plays a role, but it's him. It's on him to keep his family together. And his thang in his pants." Crystal muttered.

"Crys we need to talk."

"No we don't. I was just waiting for you to say those four words. Detective Monday and I took classes together in college. I already knew. And you did the right thing."

Jazmin looked at Crystal in astonishment. "Girl, how in the hell are you holding it together?"

If Derek has connections like that, I'm gonna play the loyal dumb wife role all the way through. They're building a case, there's no need for me to do anything other than to keep playing like I know nothing. Told you we should've left they asses in that arcade.

Chapter 2

Rescued

In the middle of the night, after continuously removing debris, the first responders and volunteers were able to pull Firemen Vega from the wreckage. He is alive, but in very bad condition. Both of his legs were broken, a broken arm, as well as his back. His airways were filled with dust and debris. As he was being lifted out, he managed to motion two fingers, indicating two more people were in that same area. Responders continued moving piles of rock until they found the body of Firemen Anthony. He was hovering in such a position as if he were a shield, protecting something or someone. Carefully, his body was exhumed and beneath him, curled in a fetal position with his helmet on, was Tasha. She was alive, but unconscious.

"Need medics ASAP! She's breathing and pregnant!" A Fireman called out.

Tasha was cautiously lifted and rushed to the hospital. She had no forms of identification on her to notify her next of kin. However, reports of survivors began to come out, and a news reporter on the scene went on air stating a pregnant woman was found and rushed to the hospital. Erica has been watching, crying and praying. When she heard the news, she picked up her phone and called Ms. Keyes.

Erica picked Tasha's mother up and made their way to the hospital as fast and as best they could. Once they arrived, it was total chaos. Apparently word got out that any and all survivors would be coming to this specific hospital and all family and friends of the victims flooded the hospital with their cares and concerns.

"How may I help you?" The nurse asked as they finally approached the front desk.

"Yes. Tasha Keyes has been admitted here. She came in a while ago from the Trade Center." Erica explained.

The nurse checked the registry. "Umm, no Ma'am. We have no one under that name admitted."

Erica looked at her evilly. "The hell you mean you don't see her name?"

The nurse, equally annoyed, replied. "Just what the hell I said! No one here under that name."

Ms. Keyes quickly interjected. "Erica, Baby let me handle this. Miss, we believe my daughter was rescued and brought here. Her name is Tasha Keye, she's 28 years old and almost nine months pregnant."

When Ms. Keyes mentioned pregnant, the nurse looked up at her with a concerned look on her face. "Please take a seat for a moment."

"What's wrong?" Erica asked.

"The doctor will be with you in a minute." The nurse replied, as she got up and went into another room.

"What happened?" Erica asked Ms. Keyes, as they sat in the waiting room.

"Let's pray all is well. God is in control."

After several minutes, the nurse returned and escorted them to a consultation room.

A doctor came into the room. "Hello, I'm Dr. Brady. You are?"

"I'm Linda Keyes, and this is Erica Goodman."

"And you say that you know the pregnant woman that was admitted?"

"Her name is Tasha. This is her mother and I'm her best friend."

Dr. Brady looked at them for a second then spoke. "Follow me."

They walked down the hall to a window looking into the Intensive Care Unit.

Both Ms. Keyes and Erica immediately recognized Tasha.

"Tasha!" Erica cried.

"Is my daughter going to be ok?"

"She is still unconscious but stable."

"Is the baby fine?" Erica asked with concern.

"Yes. With the trauma of the events, she is close enough to full term and stable enough to safely deliver the baby. The paramedics informed us she was hovered over by a fireman, with his helmet on. He gave his life to save theirs. Wait here. I'll have a nurse escort you to a private lounge area. I'll keep you updated as we progress." Dr. Brady stated.

"Thank you Doctor." Ms. Keyes said, reaching out to hug him.

Once they got comfortable in the lounge, Erica revealed something to Ms. Keyes.

"Let's not tell Shawne or Roman anything until they get here."

"Why not? Shanwe is worried sick." Ms. Keyes replied.

"I know he is. Shawne has his own issues to deal with. Perhaps not knowing Tasha's status will force him to re-evaluate himself and make some decisions."

Chapter 3

Revelations

Shawne got back to New York late Wednesday night. He could not reach Tasha nor her mother. He didn't know what to do, or who else to call. He called Travis and asked to meet with him. Travis agreed to meet with Shawne at The Diner on the Blvd.

Once Shawne arrived, Travis was there waiting in a booth already. Shawne walked over, fist bumped and hugged his former mentor. A feeling of calm suddenly came over him as they sat across from each other in the booth.

"I'm sure I know what has you worried, but this will be more effective if you tell me." Travis began.

Shawne sighed deeply. He had to unburden himself.

"No judgment Shawne. Just speak from the heart."

"When I said 'I Do', I lied. I lied to God, family and friends in attendance, my wife to be. I lied to myself. I always knew I still loved Tasha. I figured I could have the best of both since they were on opposite coasts. What I didn't bank on was lackin' love towards my wife and being suspected of it. I have a daughter who's almost six with Jazmin, and Tasha was due in less than a month with our son."

"What do you mean 'was due'? Travis asked.

Trav, she was in the Towers. No one has heard anything from her."

Being a police officer, Travis has connections Shawne didn't know about. " Hold that thought a minute." Travis gets up and goes outside to make a phone call. Five minutes later, he comes back inside. "Come on. Let's finish this on the road. I'll drive."

As they drove, Shawne continued being completely open and honest about everything he had done. Staring out the window, Shawne spoke again after a short pause. "I told Jaz I wanted a break, and my feelings for Tasha, but I hadn't told her about the baby. I know, I need to. These last few days have really put life in a different perspective for me. I've always felt a sense of being in control. Being stuck where I had no way of protecting her, no way of rescuing her and the baby. I sat there, helpless, not knowing if she was safe. If she was alive. I'm tryin' to learn to allow God to take control and leave it with Him."

"Is that what you did?" Travis challenged.

"I'm tryin'. I came to you, hopin' you would help guide me and be like an accountability partner." Shawne stated.

Travis looked over at Shawne as he pulled into a space in the hospital's parking lot. "I got you my brother. Shawne, you're about to be under attack by the Enemy and it's gonna get harder before it gets easier. Tasha is here. She's alive but in a coma."

As Shawne listened to Travis, he began to fidget his fingers and clench his fists. "My son. Is he okay?"

"Let's go inside." Travis suggests.

Once inside, Travis speaks with a nurse and identifies himself and Shawne. The nurse immediately escorts them to a lounge where they see Ms .Keyes

"Mom." Shawne says, walking towards her.

"Shawne! I'm so glad you're here!" She replied as she hugged him.

"How are you Ms. Keyes? It's me. Travis Dunbar."

"Given the circumstances, I'm well." Ms. Keyes replied.

"What's goin' on? What are the doctors sayin'?" A concerned Shawne asked.

"Tasha is stable, but still unconscious. They don't know when she'll wake up or what she will remember. But…" Ms. Keyes hesitates.

"But what Ma?"

Ms. Keyes looked at Shawne for a long moment then cracked a warm loving smile.

"My Grandson was born. September 12th, 11:55 p.m. He's small, but a healthy 5lbs 9oz. And he is so handsome."

Shawne, in amazement, slowly sat down. He was excited about the news of his son being born with no health related issues, but he also knew he had no more time to waste and decisions needed to be made. Shawne looked up at Ms. Keyes. "Can I see him?"

"Of course." She replied.

"Shawne, we'll chop it up later in the week. Like I told you. I got you. Ms. Keyes, take care. I'm praying for Tasha." Travis said.

"Aiight Trav, and thanks again."

Ms. Keyes walked Shawne down the hall to the baby ward. From the window, she pointed out his son to him. "There's my grandbaby. Ta'Shawne Nasir Thomas."

Shawne looked at her with a smile. "You knew?"

"Tasha told me early in her pregnancy, but I changed the spelling. T.A. apostrophe, capital S. If that's okay."

"That's great Ma." Shawne answered, never taking his eyes off his son.

"You need to hold him. Come on." With much excitement, Ms. Keyes led him the way.

Inside, when Shawne picked his son up for the first time, his heart melted much like it did when he first laid eyes on Kayla. He had a head full of hair, and big soft eyes. They gazed intensely at each other.

"Hey little man. Daddy's here now." Shawne said, adorning his son.

Shawne turned to Ms. Keyes. "Can I see Tasha and bring the baby in with me?"

Ms. Keyes looked at the nurse.

"Only for a brief moment." The nurse answered.

"Yes ma'am. Thank you." Shawne said following her out the room with his baby.

They stand in front of Tasha's room.

"I'm going to get a cup of coffee and then we'll have to go back." The nurse stated.

"I'm going with her, Shawne." Ms. Keyes added.

Shawne agreed and slowly went inside. Tasha was hooked up to machines. She looked like she was in a deep, peaceful sleep.

"Hey Lil Shawne, this is Mommy." He introduced, using his baby voice.

He looked down at Tasha, sighed, then spoke to her. "Tash, I'm sorry I couldn't be there for you. Watchin' the whole ordeal unfold on television, not knowin' if you made it out or not… It made me realize how much I haven't been there for you before this. But I promise you, things are about to change. I thank God for bringing you through it all. And thank you for our son. I love you Tasha!" He bent down and kissed her on the forehead. "We'll see you soon Babe." And with their baby cuddled securely in his arms, he walked out the room.

Chapter 4

Facing The Music

The League decided to postpone the second week of games. Shawne spent most of that time going to see Tasha, his son, and speaking quite often with Travis. He booked a flight home, to spend some time with Jazmin and Kayla. In LA, on Friday, Jazmin was in the office alone when Derek showed up.

"What up Jaz?" Derek spoke, standing in her office doorway.

"Derek." She nonchalantly replied.

"Look, y'all need to stop trippin'. I ain't have shit to do wit none of..."

"Don't say it! Don't talk about it! I don't wanna hear it." Jazmin interjected and warned.

"Damn. Okay." Derek laughed. He then took a seat in her office. "So let's talk about other stuff. How you been? How's my niece doin'? We don't all hang out the way we once did."

"Damn. I wonder why?" Jazmin sarcastically replied.

Derek smirked. "You really wonder why? For real?" He stared at her for a long silent moment. "How's Shawne doin' Jaz?"

"Go to hell Derek." She said through clenched teeth.

"Ooh. She said that with fire." Derek laughed again. "Naw, Imma leave you alone. I'll see ya later Jaz." Derek walked out, but stuck his head back in. "Oh by the way, I heard Tasha made it out. Congrats on the baby, StepMomma." He said then casually walked out the office.

The next evening Shawne walked through the front door where he stood before several packed suitcases and Jazmin sitting on the couch awaiting his arrival.

"What's this?" Shawne asked.

"I'm not going to raise my voice past this tone. I don't wanna fight and I don't want anymore lies." Jazmin said very calmly.

Shawne knew she knew already. He sat down across from her.

"Tasha made it out. She was pregnant with my son and he was born on the 12th." Shawne stated looking her in the eyes, in a low monotone voice.

"That's probably the first truth you have told me in years. This entire marriage was built on lies. You've been seeing her since the beginning. In turn, I found comfort in the company of another man. Funny thing is, I'm really not upset about your son. It hurts like hell, but I'm not even mad. I'll have papers drawn up. I'm keeping the house, you get the condo. Our business ventures will remain as is. I'm not out to hurt you. And I know you will always take care of Kayla. As a matter of fact, she's at Aunt Sheryl's. Your bags are already packed, let's take them over there and you can see KayKay for a little bit."

"Wait Jaz, it's just that simple? Don't I get a say-so in this?"

"Shawne, what you have to say, just isn't important to me anymore." Jazmin said then headed towards the door, carrying one of his bags.

"Damn. Deja Vu." Shawne mutters to himself.

At his aunt's house, he and Kayla went into the yard to talk as he pushed her on the swing. As they talked, Tiffany pulled into the driveway.

"Daddy, Mommy said you are moving out and that I have a little brother." Kayla said.

"So Mommy didn't let me tell you anything for myself. Yes, KayKay. It's true. Me and Mommy don't love each other the way we used to, but we both still love you."

"How much?" Kayla asked.

"Too much!" Shawne responded, making Kayla grin.

"I'm about to start playing basketball. Are you gonna come to my games?"

"Of course I am. And you can come to my games and practice when you come to visit me."

Tiffany walked out there. "Hey Auntie." Kayla said to her.

"Hey Cutey Cutey. Go inside and help Auntie Sheryl cook. Lemme talk to your daddy."

"Okay." Kayla jumped off the swing and hugged her father. "I love you Daddy."

"I love you too CoCoPop."

"Hey." Tiffany said.

"Tiff, I know you know. I know you're disappointed in me."

"Shawne, I just wanna know how we move on from here? I'm disappointed that we don't have the relationship we once did."

"There's no plan for it. We just gotta do it. I knew I was doing wrong and I knew you would call me out on it. But I'm not hidin' anymore. I'm sorry for shuttin' you out."

Tiffany opened her arms. "I love you Baby Brother." "Love you too." He replied as they embraced.

"Pull another stunt like this though, and Imma beat that ass." She said with a serious look, but then smiled.

Chapter 5

Awakened

Roman called Shawne to inform him that Tasha was awake and alert. The next day he caught a flight back to go see her. He tapped softly on the door and slowly opened it. Ms. Keyes was there with Tasha, as she cradled her baby boy.

"Hey." Shawne said, walking in.

"Hey." Ms. Keyes replied, getting up to hug him.

Shawne stepped towards Tasha's bed, stroked her hair, and kissed her on the forehead.

"I felt so helpless, Tash." He softly said, adorning her.

Tasha looked at her mother. Ms. Keyes walked over to her.

"I'll take the baby to the nursery and feed him. Come to Gamma, Doodlebug." Ms. Keyes said, scooping up Lil' Ta'Shawne into her arms.

Tasha slid over a bit so Shawne could sit on the edge of the bed. After Tasha's mother left the room, Tasha grabbed a hold of his hand. "Let's talk Shawne." She said in a groggy, but clear voice. Shawne turned very attentively towards her.

"That horrific event…" She closed her eyes, reimagining the day. She takes a deep breath. "That day will be forever remembered in history books. But for me, the experience of it… It's like a reoccurring nightmare. Feeling the ground shake and crumble from under you, walls crashing down. To know you're gonna die…"

"Tasha, Baby you're a fighter. You survived."

"I'm here by the grace of God, those two angels disguised as firemen, and the tireless efforts of the first responders and volunteers. But I thought I was going to die. And all I could think about was you, and our unborn son. Then as I slept, I knew God spared me, and I needed to start living for Him."

"I prayed too. Askin', pleadin' for God to protect you and the baby. Tasha, I told Jaz about..."

"We're moving down south Shawne. Me, Mommy and the baby." Tasha interrupted.

Shawne looked at her with a bit of confusion. He slowly gets up from the bed to process what he just heard.

"What? Down south like Trenton or Willingboro?" He asked.

"No Shawne. Like Georgia."

"So what, you woke up from the coma and said 'let's move down south.' Tasha, really?"

"No. It's actually been a consideration for quite a while. I don't want my son.."

"Our son." Shawne cut in.

"I don't want our son to be raised here. I didn't know if or when you were ever gonna step up and handle your business. Then to top it off, your friend, Derek, he's been following me. He don't know I know. But I know."

"What?" Shawne surprisingly asked.

"After the whole Mike ordeal, I became much more aware of my surroundings. When I see an unfamiliar car in front of my place, that's one thing. But when that same vehicle is parked across the street from Mommy's house. That ain't a coincidence. I made a police report, but I knew that wouldn't go far without more proof, so we hired someone to check into it."

"Why didn't you tell me?" Shawne asked.

"At first, I didn't know if you had him doing it. Then I figured it was probably your wife's doing. Mommy stayed paranoid, so one night we were talking and decided we would move back to Atlanta."

"Tasha, I told Jazmin all about us and the baby."

"Shawne." She says, closing her eyes and sighing. For months, you had the opportunity to straighten out your affairs. But you stayed on the fence, fearing that you'd lose one. Trying to play it safe. Shawne, we're leaving sooner than later. Ta'Shawne is your son, and I'd never keep him from you. But the decision has already been made."

Shawne was clearly upset but he had to contain it. He didn't want to upset Tasha. "When?" He pouted and rolled his eyes.

"Next month." She replied.

Shawne walked over to the window and stared out. "What does this mean for us?"

"Right now, I gotta focus on me. You need to focus on you. And together, but separately, we need to focus on our son."

Shawne continued looking out the window, and his temper slowly began to boil. All the while, Tasha continued to talk, thinking he was being understanding.

"And you need to get back focused on football." Tasha stated lastly. Shawne turned around. "You know what Tasha? Fuck football! You bringin' up football when I'm losin' everything anyway! I'll talk to you later." He sternly spoke, sucking his teeth, and stormed out the room.

Chapter 6

Catchin' Hell

For days, Shawne was furious. Angry at the world because Tasha was not only moving away and taking his son, but also because she decided they would not be in a relationship. It was affecting his play on the field. They lost a 2nd straight game to start the season. Roman sat down to talk with Shawne after a terrible practice.

"Bro, I know how you feel…"

"Naw Ro. You really don't. Everything in your life is on point. You straight. Me though, I'm catchin' hell from every which way. My marriage is about to be over. Tasha is bouncin', takin' my son away. I'm gonna see even less of Kayla than I already do. To top it off, I'm playin' like shit, the media sayin' I lost it. That I ain't hungry no more."

"Is that what you think of yourself?" Roman asked.

"It don't matter what I think of myself, it's what they sayin'." Shawne whined.

"Yo." Roman gets up and walks to the opposite side of the lockers, and faces Shawne. "What happened to my dude? You feared nothin'. Didn't care what was said, just handled business. You were always certain of yourself. On the field, calm and cool in all situations. Off the field, did whateva you set your mind to. Cali, keepin' it real wit you, as an adult, you've never had to face any real life adversities. I wouldn't be a friend if

22

I didn't tell you the truth. You can't do the things you've done and not expect karma to come back on you?"

"So what you sayin' Ro? That I deserve to not see my kids? That Tasha should move away? Jaz should divorce me? I deserve it?" Shawne questioned.

"Friend to friend, naw Bro. I'd never say you deserve any of that. I know you're a great father and that'll never change. But you've scorned two women. Shawne, you told your wife you loved another woman, and strung Tasha along until she just gave up hope. We all reap what we sow."

Shawne couldn't see the forest for the trees. He could not take Roman's words as constructive criticism.

"I don't know Dog, sounds like you takin' the opportunity to say '*I told you so, Cali*'. With the bullshit about reaping what I sow."

Roman just stared at his friend with a bewildered look.

"Wow. Erica was right. You don't wanna own your mess ups." Roman began to walk away before things got heated between them.

"Fuck you mean Erica was right? She don't know shit…"

Roman interrupted him, turning back to him, speaking more sternly.

"Don't do it Shawne! Feel how you want about what I said, but don't disrespect my wife! You wanna sit on ya pity pot and feel like the world is against you? That's on you. But me and Erica always had ya back." Roman and Shawne stood there, face to face, for what seemed like an eternity, neither backing down.

"You need help. Talk to Travis. I got nothin' else for you. Peace, Shawne." Roman turned and walked out.

A few days later, Shawne was home and decided to call Tasha. He hadn't spoken to her since he stormed out of the hospital, nor had he seen his son.

"Hello?" Tasha answered.

"Hey. How you feelin'?" Shawne replied.

"Wow. What a surprise." Tasha sarcastically began. "I'm better. I'm up and moving around since coming home." She answered, holding the between her ear and shoulder, while she held Ta'Shawne, and fed him.

"Yeah, I'm sorry I haven't been by, but I got some free time now. I can come pick y'all up and stay the night."

"You can come by Mommy's and spend time with your son. I can't come there or stay the night." Tasha replied.

"Tasha, why not?"

"Because Shawne. I meant what I said. You can see Ta'Shawne whenever, I won't deny you that. But you and I, we can't go there, Shawne."

"Go where? I just wanna spend time with y'all." Shawne tried to convince.

"Shawne, I can't. I can't be around you, alone. I know I will give into to you. Right now, that's not what's best. We're at Mommy's, you're welcome to come by."

Shawne hated rejection. "Yeah aiight. Lemme check on a few things and I'll hit you back in a few." He nonchalantly replied.

"Whateva Shawne Thomas. Save the bullshit. If it ain't your way, it's no way. I already know you ain't comin'. Your son doesn't deserve this version of you. You are so concerned about being alone, instead of trying to build that much needed relationship with him right now. You'd rather stay away, keepin' a safe distance, and act like you're tryin', when all along you're just thinkin' of yourself, protectin' your heart and feelings. Less than two weeks. Eleven days to be exact. I hope you get it together before then. Take care." Tasha hung up the phone.

Shawne plopped down on the couch and sighed deeply. He waited several minutes, then opened his phone to make another call.

"Hello?"

"How are you?"Shawne replied.

"Shawne, Kayla is at practice. What do you want?" Jazmin asked.

"I'm just checkin' on you."

Jaz chuckled. "So now you wanna check on me? Tasha must be unavailable. Or perhaps she came to her senses as well and left your ass alone. Damn, the great Shawne with an E is catchin' L's. On the field. With his wife. His mistress. Losing both kids. As bad as I wanna feel for you, I don't. You get what you give. I can't stroll down memory lane with you right now, I'm getting ready for a date tonight. If you wanna talk to your daughter, she'll be with my mom. Good night." Jaz said, then hung up.

Shawne set his phone down,walked over to the bar and poured himself a glass of Hennessy. He went and picked his phone back up, and made yet another call. He got Travis' voicemail. "What's up Trav? Hey Man, I'm really catchin' it over here. Can we meet tomorrow and talk?...

Chapter 7

The Confrontation

The next day Shawne met with Travis in his office at the church. Travis could see defeat in Shawne's eyes, in his posture. Even the words he spoke.

"Shawne, I never told anyone this, but before I met you, when I heard you were coming to Lincoln, I was actually afraid you would take my spot. I saw some of your games in the youth league. So that time, when I saw you walking through the neighborhood, I figured if I put some fear in this Freshman's heart, he would know who runnin' things. Honestly though, other than the fact there were more of us, and you were alone, I don't recall you being afraid. I'm saying this to say, since I've known you, you have always handled tough situations with poise. This is no different. You gotta stand firm in your storm, knowing God will never leave nor forsake you."

"Trav, I know, but it's easier said than done. I wanna give all this drama I caused to God and let him handle it in His just time, but keepin' it real, it just doesn't seem to fit in the timeframe I want it done."

"His time ain't our time Shawne. Spend more time in prayer and reading your bible. You're gonna suffer more. Everyone wants the joy that comes in the morning, without the pains and heartache through the night."

Shawne respected Travis for being so open and honest with him. He didn't sugarcoat it, nor did he flatout tell Shawne he was wrong for all he had done. Shawne knew he had to figure out how he would better handle all his messy situations.

Shawne had an away game in Chicago. They won, but still, he and Roman are not speaking, they have no connection on the field either. There were rumors swirling around the locker room that Roman wanted to be traded.

Shawne and Bo are sitting at the bar in the hotel talking.

"How much longer will you and Ro keep this up?"

"This what he wanted. It's what he chose." Shawne stated.

"Shawne, y'all not speaking affects more people than just the two of you. Both on and off the field. I know y'all just kinda took the Rookie in at first, and y'all been tight for years. But both y'all became my brothers. The connection we created was like no other I ever had in my life."

Bo's conversation with Shawne was interrupted by a slow hand clap. They both turn around in unison. Standing behind them was Derek, along with his boys Con and Lock.

"That was beautiful. It almost brought a tear to my eye, but then I remembered who you're talkin' about. Shawne don't give a damn about nobody not named Shawne. Trust me, I know. I was his best friend since we was what... six?"

Shawne looks at Bo. "Aye Bo, lemme holla at them. I'll catch up to you in a bit."

"Yeah Bo, let us kick it wit the Homie for a lil while." Derek reiterated.

Bo looked at the three men standing, then at his quarterback. "Naw Bro, he is my business. I got his back, they got yours." Bo stood up and stood behind Shawne's stool so Derek could sit down. Derek looked at Shawne as he sat.

"You heard the man. He got my back." Shawne said.

"So this the game you wanna play Cuz?"

"I don't know what you're talkin' about. I ain't the one playin' games. You havin' Tasha followed. And I know you told Jaz about the baby." Shawne said.

Derek smirked. "That's petty shit Homey. Now the shit you did… Nigga, you broke the code. The Homies here were ready to handle either one or both of them for what you did. But I said naw, let's wait and see what he has to say first."

"Say about what?" Shawne asked with aggravation.

"Shawne. Everybody knows you talked with One Time."

"Oh, so because the police called me in for questioning, what, I snitched? So call yourself gettin' some getback by rattin' me out to my wife? Man Derek, fuck you! Since day one, I always looked out for you! Always looked out for you! I don't owe you jack shit, but before I walk away from this conversation and you forever, lemme say this. I never met any females you dealt with while you been married. And I only know these two by street names. So whateva shit y'all into, has nothin' to do with me. I can't throw you no more life savers. You on ya own from here on. If anything happens to anyone connected to me… You know the Hulk in me you used to speak about? Well Imma beat his ass senseless on my way to get at you three muthafuckas! Let's roll Bo."

Shawne got up, brushed past Con and Lock, as Bo followed.

"Aye yo D, what's up? Let's go handle that Nigga!" Con said.

Derek thought momentarily, then shook his head. "Naw, stall him out. He ain't say nothin' to the cops."

28

Chapter 8

Moving On & Away

Another game, another loss for Shawne. In his post-game interview with reporters, he was short, nonchalant and pouty. His demeanor read as though it was everyone's fault but his own. He was the last to leave the locker room. Outside, leaned up against his car, stood Roman. Shawne stopped and stared. "What's up?" He asked dryly.

"We haven't talked in a minute. I hate that we beefin', and I'm not even sure if it's business or personal. But either way, the point where we at right now, yo, this shouldn't be us. We've always been bigger than this."

"You right. Things never been like this between us."Shawne replied.

"I want you to hear this from me and not any other source. I got new representation, and we went to the GM asking for a trade." Roman stated to Shawne.

Although Shawne heard rumors swirling around, it was a shock to hear Roman tell him that. "You gotta do what's best for you and yours right?" You know Tasha leaves tomorrow. Have you spoken to her? Have you seen your Lil' Man?"

Shawne sighed deeply, then looked away as tears began to well up in his eyes.

"Go see them Bro." Roman said, stepping towards him.

Pawing aways tears, Shawne sidestepped Roman and opened his car door. "Yeah. Aiight. I will. I'll holla at you later Ro." Shawne said in a crackling voice, fighting back tears. Never looking at Roman, he got into his vehicle, started and slowly backed out, as Roman watched his friend struggle.

That evening, Shawne called his family. Aunt Sheryl, Tiffany. Then Jazmin, to check on Kayla. "Hey Jaz. How are you? He began.

"I'm good, and you?"

He sighs. I'm tryin'" "How's your son and baby mama?"

"Jaz, please don't start on me. Can I talk with Kayla?" Shawne begged.

"Kay Kay, phone for you."

"Hello?"

"Wow! You sound so big! Are you growing up on me?"

"Hi Daddy. When are you coming home? Daddy, you gotta see me play. My coach says that I'm really good. You gotta come home. Please?" She begged.

"Soon Baby. Real soon."

"You promise Daddy?"

"I promise Daughter. I love you Kay-Kay."

"I love you too. Mommy wants you."

She handed the phone back to her mother.

"Were you planning to come out next weekend?"

"Yeah, why?"

"Because she'll be at my mom's. I'm going away for the weekend."

"What you mean, you're goin' away for the weekend?" Shawne demanded to know.

Jazmin laughed. "Baby you gave that privilege up when you chose the other chick. Better yet, goodbye Shawne. We're not doing this." Jaz said and hung up.

Shawne, through clenched teeth, inhaled and puffed heavily, as he hung up the phone.

He picked the phone back up, and began dialing Tasha's number, but hung up, grabbed his jacket and headed out the door.

He drove to Ms. Keys' house. Shawne parked across and down the street. He grabbed the handle to open the door and get out but he froze. Shawne looked at the side view mirror at the house. He released the door, closed his eyes and began reminiscing about the day of Tasha's senior prom. His mom, dad and little sister were there. Eyes still closed, he sighed deeply, as a tear ran down his cheek. "It wasn't supposed to be this way." He mumbled to himself. Shawne sat there recalling the past so long, he fell asleep. He was awakened by the vibration of his pager. He yawned and stretched open his eyes to read a text from Tasha.

'Shawne, I can't believe you have let the fact that I'm moving away get in the way of you spending time with your son. I'll give you the benefit of the doubt. I know you got alot going on. We're leaving soon... My number ain't changing. Ta'Shawne is ready for his daddy. The longer you wait, the harder it'll be Shawne. As for you and I... I really believed that love began and ended with you. I was willing to do whatever it took to get you and keep you, just for me. Then when you showed me you weren't willing to do the same, I blamed you. I'm sorry for doing so. Your place was with your family, and I came in between that. I realized my fault and nearly paid for it with my life and our son's life. But God saw fit to spare my life, moreso, Lil' Shawne's. Jazmin may never forgive me, but I'm truly apologetic for putting her through all this.*

Shawne, unguard your heart and let your son in, please? I'll always love you, Number 11.'

Once he finished reading the text message, he looked in the rearview and saw Ms. Keys getting into the vehicle, and Tasha strapping the baby in the backseat. After she closed the door, she stood in the street and stretched, also reminiscing her times growing up on that street, in that house. She looked back towards where Shawne was parked. She stared in his direction and he looked back, thinking she saw him. Tasha then closed her eyes, turned and got in the car to drive off. Shawne just stared, as they drove away.

Chapter 9

The Unraveling Continues

At the Bye Week, New York was 2 and 4, Shawne was playing the worst football ever in his life, his once best friend was traded to Atlanta of all places. And his teammate Bo Cornbeef Dane was out for the season with a torn ACL.

Shawne packed a bag and headed to Los Angeles for the weekend. Once he arrived, he caught a cab to the house. His key didn't work, so he rang the bell. He then called Jazmin, but her phone went to voicemail. He flagged the cabbie before he left the driveway and went to his mother-in-law's house. Ms. Davis was parking as the cab arrived. When Shawne got out, Kayla, sitting in the backseat, turned and saw him and screamed in excitement.

"Daddy!" She yelled, getting out and running to leap into his arms. She hugged his neck so tightly.

Shawne choked on tears as he squeezed his daughter. "I missed you so, so much!"

"Mommy didn't tell me you were coming."

"Where is she? Is she in the house?"

Kayla shook her head. "I think she is with Mr. Stephon."

"Who?" Shawne asked as his heart dropped.

"Her friend, Mr. Stephon. She said he works with you and Uncle Derek." Kayla continued.

Ms. Davis interrupted. "Kay-Kay Baby, take this in the house for me?"

"Ok-K."Kayla said as she took the bag and ran into the house.

She looked at her son-in-law with a bit of pity. "I don't condone what either of you have done, and I'm not siding with her because she's my daughter. You're my son as well. But did you really expect her to sit around and wait for you? Son, you hurt her. You hurt her to her core."

Shawne lowered his head in shame. "Where is she now?"

"I'm not sure. Shawne, come inside. Spend time with your daughter." She suggested to her son-in-law.

Shawne agreed and went in. While watching television with his mother-in-law and Kayla. Shawne texted Harper, asking him to call as soon as possible. Harper called back within a minute of Shawne's text. He excused himself and went out to the backyard.

"Harp, what's up?"

"I kinda figured you would be calling me soon."

"So you know what's goin' with Jaz?"

"Derek wanted me to delete some files. I came in and overheard Jazmin talking on the phone. At the time, I couldn't say for sure who she was talking to, but I knew you would want to know. So I began looking into it."

"Stephon again?" Shawne solemnly asked.

"Yeah man. I'm sorry. It seems serious too. It's been about a month now."

34

"Do me a favor. Come pick me up from Jaz's mom's house."

Harp agreed and they hung up. Shawne went back inside, sat on the couch and his daughter climbed onto his lap and kissed his cheek.

"Is everything alright?" Ms. Davis asked.

Shawne nodded. "Yes. A friend of mine is gonna come get me to go see Auntie."

"I wanna go Daddy." Kayla interjected.

"Okay, but first I gotta go handle some business. I'll come back and get you."

He looked at Ms. Davis, as she gave him a suspicious look. "Shawne." She warned.

"I'm good Mom, I just gotta hang with the fellas for a little while. Clear my head, then I'll be back to scoop this lil nugget up." He said, tickling his baby girl.

As he played with Kayla, a horn honked twice outside. Shawne looked towards the door. "Aiight. I'll be back in a bit. Love you KayPop."

"Love you too Daddy." Kayla replied.

Anita stood up and hugged her estranged son in law. "Listen to me Shawne. It's not too late. It's never too late to make something right. I'm praying for you. Both of you."

It was hard for Shawne to look her in the eye after those words from her because he knew how strongly Ms. Davis advocated for him and Jaz. "I love you Mom." He said and headed to the door. Kayla followed him and watched him get in the car from the front window. As Harper drove away, Shawne waved goodbye to Kayla.

"Aiight Harp, what's the deal Bro?"

"Well like I said, they've been back in constant contact for a while now. I don't know how it started back up, but it's going pretty strong."

Shawne listened as he looked out the window, imagining Stephon having sex with his wife. He sniffles and rubs his eyes. "Do you know where she is now? Shawne asked.

Harper pulled the car over, and pulled a GPS tracking device out from the center console. He handed it to Shawne.

"What's this?"

"Press the power button to turn it on." Harp said.

Shawne did so, and after several minutes of uploading, two icons appeared on the screen.

"That's Derek. And that's Mrs. Thomas. I put trackers on both cars. Like I said, I knew this call was coming. And tracking Derek was in the best of both interests."

"Where are they now?" Shawne asked.

Harp looked at it. "Derek is in y'all old neighborhood. He's been staying over there since he and Crystal separated."

"They separated?" Shawne asked surprisingly.

"You didn't know?"

"No. Hadn't spoken to either of them lately."

"Derek is looking at some serious charges." Harp stated.

"That's on him. I got my own issues. Where's Jaz on this thing?"

Harper looked at Shawne. She looks to be headed in the direction of your house."

Shawne got an uneasy feeling in his gut. "Take me."

"Shawne, do you think…"

"Take me and drop me off around the corner, then disappear. She won't know you have anything to do with this." Shawne interrupted.

Harper took a deep breath and obliged.

Once they arrived, Shawne reassured Harper everything would be fine. He got out of the car and walked towards the house, while Harper turned in the opposite direction and drove away. As he approached the driveway, he saw that Crystal's car was there. He knocked at the door in a polite manner.

"I'll get it." Crystal called out being closest to the front door. She opened it to see Shawne, much to her surprise. "Sha…"

"Where that nigga at?" Shawne ignored her as he brushed past Crystal to go inside. "Jaz! Your crazy ass husband is here!" Crystal yelled.

Jazmin met Shawne in the livingroom. "Shawne, why are you here?"

"This my house! I pay the mortgage! Where ole boy at?" He demanded to know as he stormed past her and began searching for him. Meanwhile, Crystal subtly made a phone call.

"Where your punkass hidin' at? Come out and see me man to man!"

The women followed behind him. "Shawne, you're being a maniac!" Jaz stated.

"Jaz stop playin' me for a fool! I know the deal. You be havin'this nigga around my daughter? She callin him Uncle!"

"You have the nerve to be spyin' on me with all the shit you've done?"

"No! Kay-Kay told me got dammit!" He yelled in her face, then turned and punched the wall behind him. He snatched his hand out and knew right away he had broken it. Shawne winced in pain as he attempted to make a fist. "Shit!" He yelled in frustration.

Just then, two police officers with guns drawn, entered the front door of the residence. Crystal left it open and her anonymous call was a 911 call.

"I need everyone to calm down and listen to me." One officer said as the two found Shawne, Jazmin, and Crystal in the hallway, near the master bedroom.

"The hell y'all doin' in my house? Guns out and shit!" Shawne snapped.

"Mr. Thomas. Turn around, go to your knees, cross your legs and place your hands on your head."

"For what? I'm in my house!"

"Ladies, come this way please." The second officer instructed.

Jazmin and Crystal obliged.

"Again, Mr. Thomas. Please turn around, go to your knees, cross your legs, and place your hands on your head. Sir Please!" The first officer stated in a stronger tone.

Shawne looked at Jazmin. "So this is really what it's come to?"

Jazmin began to feel a slight bit of sympathy. "Shawne please, do as they ask you." She pleaded.

Shawne, still holding his right hand, stared a long moment at his estranged wife, then slowly, turned around and followed the officer's instructions.

The first officer gave the second a head nod to cuff Shawne. The officer grabbed Shawne's hand and he screamed in pain, falling forward to the floor.

"He broke his hand, he isn't resisting!" Jaz tried to explain.

The second officer placed his knee on Shawne's back, while the first officer moved closer. He holstered his gun, squatted down to hold Shawne's legs. "His hand is possibly broken. Cuff him, but in front."

The officers got up and assisted Shawne to his feet. "Hold your wrist out, palms up. Adam-14 to Dispatch. Start medics to our location. Everything is 10-4. Needed for a possible broken hand." The first officer stated on the radio as he placed the cuffs on Shawne.

As Shawne was escorted to the patrol vehicle, he just stared at Jazmin.

"One of the neighbors must have heard him." Jazmin said to Crystal.

"No. I dialed when he came in like a wild man. J, I didn't know what he was gonna do."

Shawne calmly sat in the back of the squad car. Watching Jazmin and Crystal talking to the police as they awaited the ambulance to arrive. He then closed his eyes and a tear ran down his cheek. Shawne felt like he just hit the lowest point of his life. From being the golden kid everyone loves, winning championships at every level, having a supportive family and great friends. Being the top pick in the draft, a husband and father. To now, a questionable leader on the field, losing both of his best friends, a cheater. A cheater, an absentee father of two children with two women he claims he loves but could never fully show one of them true unconditional love. All these thoughts and emotions circumvented within as he sat in that back seat possibly awaiting to go to jail.

"Lord, again, I find myself living outside of Your Will. I wanna confess my sins to you and apologize, but that ain't enough. I want forgiveness from You and everyone I've hurt and am hurting. But I don't know how to forgive myself. Father, I don't wanna be angry anymore. I accept my role, my faults in all that has gone wrong. Forgive me Lord. Teach me to forgive myself as well. I accept whatever pains and punishments I face because of my actions. And I will live to glorify Your Holy Name. I will strive to be better daily, and I know I'll need help. Please God, hold me now. I'm weak. Help make me strong. Bring strong influences in my life, and the ones already a part, make them stronger. I love you, I thank you, and I ask this all in the Loving Name of Your Son, Jesus Christ. Amen."

When he opened his eyes, the ambulance was pulling up, and the officer was opening the door. "Step out Mr. Thomas please sir. Your wife and friend explained what happened and this will be written up as a domestic dispute only." The officer said as he removed the cuffs.

"Will I have to go to court or pay any fines?" Shawne asked.

"No Sir. Let's just get this hand checked out for you."

The ambulance drove Shawne to hospital, where he had x-rays performed. Shawne had a fractured knuckle. The doctor told him he would not require surgery, but would be sidelined for 3 to 4 weeks.

Jazmin drove Shawne home. "Let's talk Shawne." Jazmin said.

"Ok." He replied very calmly.

Jazmin didn't speak until she pulled into the driveway of the house.

"Do you have any idea how much you hurt me?" She began.

Shawne lowered his head and sighed. "I do. I know you think you had a good man in me, because I provided for you. And I thought that was enough. But physically, emotionally, spiritually, I failed you. I failed Kayla. I'm failing a son whom I don't know. I hurt you because you're a good woman that deserves to be placed on a pedestal and honored. I think of how my father did that with my mom, and cherished his kids. Somewhere along the way, I lost focus of that, and that's on me, and it hurts more now because finally, I'm looking at me through your eyes." Shawne said, looking up at her.

Jazmin's eyes quickly began to well up with tears. She knew why she hadn't yet proceeded with a divorce. She was still deeply in love with Shawne.

"Shawne, about Stephon I ran into him a month ago…"

Shawne reached over and kissed his wife's forehead. "You deserve to be happy. No explanations. I love you Jazzy, still." He got out of the car, and softly closed the door. He squatted to look at her still in the car, now crying, and mouthed "Forever. I'm sorry I hurt you." He stood up and slowly walked away. Jazmin sat there, crying her eyes out as her husband disappeared in the night.

Shawne called Harper to pick him up and take him back to his mother-in-law's. Once he got there she was waiting at the door. He hugged her and kissed her cheek. He then went upstairs to Kayla's room, got into bed and laid there, with her in his arms until he fell asleep.

Chapter 10

The Dawn of a New Day

Shawne sat out a month with his injury, and he lost his starting position in the process with the team responding better to the back-up QB. Shawne graciously accepted his new role. He knew he had to win back the trust of the team, coaches, the organization as a whole, as well as the fanbase. He has been meeting with Travis regularly for counseling sessions ever since his return to New York after fracturing his hand.

"How does your hand feel?" Travis asked him as they left-hand fist bumped to greet one another.

"I feel tightness in it, but it's coming around."

"You gonna be ready if your number gets called?"

Shawne hunched his shoulders with a careless look.

"Wow." Travis said.

"What?" Shawne asked, with a confused look.

"This isn't you. I'm not used to it. I don't see that competitive fire in you that you've always had."

Shawne looked around Travis' office. "I don't know if I love it the same as I used to. Football was always my first love. Everything else came in second." Shawne thought momentarily about what he said before speaking again. "I guess that's where I went wrong. No one or nothin' else mattered enough to me to be put before football."

"Keep goin' Brotha." Travis encouraged.

Shawne continued in thought, slowly speaking the words he thought. "Football was good to me, but I used it to hurt others around me." He looked at Travis in his eyes. "The more successful I became, the more football became my god." He shamefully admitted.

"Mmmm! That's deep Shawne. Now you're starting to see. We all fall to something, somewhere, somehow. But we all don't recognize our faults, and when we do…"

"We don't always correct them and grow from them either." Shawne continued.

"The fact that you're finishing my sentences, tells me you're ready and growing."

"Trav, I disappointed so many people. My moms and pops would be disappointed too."

"Shawne, God has forgiven you. You have to forgive yourself so you can ask for forgiveness from the people you've hurt. Hurt people hurt people. As long as you carry the sorrowful weight of your past, you can never ask anyone to forgive you, because you can't forgive yourself. Forgiveness isn't even for them. It's for you. When you ask for forgiveness, it'll reflect in the way you carry yourself after that. If the other person can't accept it, that burden falls on them." Travis stated.

"Give it to God. Leave it with God." Shawne said, then reminisced.

"There's power in that simple saying."

"Yeah. I remember my mom sayin' to me; If it's meant to be, let it go." Shawne smiled.

"Yep. What is meant, will be." Travis stated.

Shawne didn't play anymore the rest of the season. He slowly but surely continued to work on himself. He was attending church services more. He read scriptures more and prayed quite often. He was finally finding peace within himself and rebuilding his relationship with God, but he had yet to make amends with Jazmin or Tasha. He hadn't heard from Roman, and moreso, he hadn't spoken much to Kayla and hadn't seen his son, Ta'Shawne who was now almost 5 months old.

Shawne didn't have an agent at this time either since he and Derek were also on the outs. One morning he got a call from the general manager informing him he was about to be traded to Houston.

When Shawne hung up the phone, his heart sank. He was being traded to the worst team in the league for a 5th round pick. He took that as a slap in the face. Just a year ago, he led this franchise back to prominence and brought a championship title to the city. He felt betrayed, but rather than get angry, he closed his eyes to find peace within. "What is meant, will be." He muttered to himself.

Chapter 11

Judged by 12, Carried by 6

A month before training camp, Shawne has comfortably settled into his new apartment in downtown Houston. He was watching the news and saw that Derek's murder trial started. He hated what had become of their friendship. He wanted to call, but he knew it was best that he stayed away from that whole ordeal. But he would follow the coverage closely. Shawne flipped over to a sports network and saw his other once best friend, Roman got injured running routes with his teammates. He tore ligaments in his knee and will miss the entire season. "Damn." He sighed. Shawne picked his cell phone up and texted Roman.

He didn't expect Roman to reply, which he didn't. He thought back to his high school days, and recalled his mentor, Coach Brown. Shawne jumped up, got dressed and drove out to Coach's house.

He pulled up, the home looked abandoned. The grass was overgrown, no vehicles in the driveway, and the chair Coach sat in when he and Roman came was overturned on the porch. Shawne looked through the contacts on his phone and called Coach's daughter, Andrea.

"Hello?" She answered.

"Hey Andrea? It's Shawne. Is everything ok? I drove out here to the house."

"Hey Shawne." She sighs. "No. Daddy has been really sick. I had to put him in a home. He has been in and out of the hospital. Me and the boys moved into an apartment closer to the home he was in. I've just been too busy to keep the house up and sell it."

"Where is he now?" Shawne asked.

"Memorial Hospital. But Shawne…"

"What?"

"His condition worsens daily. The doctor encourages visits but he barely recognizes even me and the boys." Andrea sobbed.

"I'm headed there now. I'll talk to you later."

He rushed over to the hospital. Visiting hours were almost over, but Shawne pleaded with the nurse to allow him to see Coach, and she gave in to him.

Shawne slowly opened the door and heard Coach Brown breathing heavily.

"Come in here boy. What took you so long to get here?" Coach Brown said, still in his deep raspy voice.

"Hey Coach, it's me, Shawne."

"Thomas, I know. Andrea told me you were coming. Sit down Son."

Shawne pulled a chair up next to him. Coach never looked up or even opened his eyes.

"Thomas, I know I've told you this before. Son, you were the best player I've coached, and Goodman as well. Coaching kids is a calling from God. Any level after high school it's a job. High school and younger, you have opportunities to mold lost boys into leaders of men."

"Yes Sir." Shawne agreed.

"What happened to you Thomas?" Coach asked him directly.

Shawne still knew Coach Brown was no nonsense. If he was asking, he already knew and you better be honest with him.

"Coach, I've been selfish and self serving. But I'm workin' on myself to be a better person."

"A better husband and father?" Coach challenged.

"I'm pretty sure my wife is done with me."

"No no no Son. She is hurting because of your actions. Has she moved completely on from you?"

"Sir, I'm really not sure."

"Son, when a woman is done, she is done. You still have the opportunity to make it right. Your children, they should not be punished for what you've done. I know you were raised better than to turn away from them. Your parents were great examples of what a mother and father should be." Coach Brown in a coughing but stern voice stated.

Shawne sat in shame. He could do nothing but agree.

"And you as well, Coach. Like you said, you molded boys into men. Any good characteristics in me, it's because you played such an influential role in my life. I hate that I've let you down. My parents down."

"Thomas. Son, life's a learning experience. You're young. Make it right. I'm very proud of you. But promise me you will step up and lead, the way God calls for you to. My time left here on earth, molding boys into strong men, is coming to an end. I held on this long to make sure my Quarterback knows what plays to call from here on out. Will you lead Son?" Coach asked, reaching to grasp Shawne's hand.

Shawne's eyes quickly watered up and he struggled to swallow, as he looked down at their hands clasped together. "I promise." He managed to say.

"Gracious and wonderful Father, Lord, we thank you for forgiveness. We thank you for never fully letting go of us when we fall. Father, my prayer right now is that this young man, Shawne Thomas continues on the path to honoring You, giving You all the glory and praise. That he steps back up in his role as strong, loyal, loving friend, husband and father. He lost his way Lord, but with prayer and guidance, Father, he is ready. I thank You Lord, for allowing me to play a role in this young man's life. Though it was through football, it's never been about football. I thank you for trusting me with every young man that has come into my life. I pray that you received all the glory. I know my time is near Father. To be absent from the body, is to be present with You, oh Lord. As always, Your Will be done. Bless us Lord. In the loving Name of Your Son, Jesus Christ. Amen."

"Amen. I love you Coach." Shawne cried, unable to hold back tears.

He hugged the big guy and then sat there in silence while Coach Brown peacefully slept. After several more minutes the nurse came in and told Shawne it was getting late. He got up, looked at his coach once more and walked out.

The next morning, Shawne woke up and called Jazmin.

"Hey Shawne. Kay-Kay is still sleeping."

"Good morning. I figured she would. I was just calling to check on you. How are you?" He asked.

"Umm, I'm good. Thanks for asking." She replied, a bit puzzled.

"I'm flying out next week, I was wondering if I could bring Kayla back for the weekend. Give both you and mom a bit of a break.

"Uh... Yeah, I guess that'll be fine."

"Cool. Can you have her give me a call when she wakes up?"

"I will. Is everything ok Shawne?"

"Yes. We'll talk. Enjoy your day Jaz." He said, then hung up.

Shawne took a deep breath, then picked the phone up again and dialed a number.

"Well. It's alive."

"Tasha…"

"Tasha nothin' Shawne! I never in a million years would think you would turn your back on your son. Hate me all you want for whateva reason."

"Tasha, I don't hate you. Yes I was angry, but I was wrong. I knew all along I was but I couldn't admit it. I couldn't face you, your mom, Lil Shawne. I couldn't face myself and deal with the situation. I thought I lost you. Then I was even more angry when I was ready to fully commit to you, but you no longer wanted us. It was selfish of me, but I knew no other way to get over you but to stay away from you. I realize it cost me precious time with our son I can never get back, but if you're willing to let me back into his life. I've gotten past the past."

"Shawne, I can't let you back into his life… You never left. He's been waiting on his daddy. Hold on. Ta'Shawne, say hi Daddy." Tasha said in a soft voice to her son.

Shawne could hear his son trying to speak. "Da… Da"

"Hey Man… Daddy is coming to see you soon." He said smiling, ear to ear.

He and Tasha talked on the phone for a while longer, discussing when he would travel to Atlanta to see them. Then the other line beeped. He clicked over. It was Andrea. She called to tell him Coach Brown passed away in his sleep a few minutes ago. Shawne clicked over, crying, telling Tasha the sad news and that he would call her back.

When he hung up, he got a text from Roman thanking him for reaching out. Shawne texted him back with the news of Coach.

Coach's homegoing service was scheduled for the following Saturday. So Shawne flew out to LA on Monday morning. His Aunt Sheryl picked him up at the airport.

"How are you feeling Baby?" She asked her nephew.

"Been better, but I'll make it through." He replied quite confidently.

His aunt smiled. "I hadn't seen this Shawne in quite some time."

"Yeah, I'm workin through my shhh, stuff." Shawne almost slipped.

Aunt Sheryl looked at him, then back at the road. "Alright now Boy. You ain't too old for me to whup you. Have you spoken to your wife? Does she know you're here?"

"She knew I was coming, but I haven't talked to her since last week." Shawne replied.

"Shawne, how do you expect to make a marriage work with no communication? And when will I see the baby?"

Tasha moved to Atlanta. As soon as I can work out arrangements with her, I'll bring Lil Shawne out here. And I know, marriage can't work without communication. I'm giving her the space she needs away from me. If she's still my wife at all."

"Don't speak negativity into your marriage. You made mistakes, she's made mistakes. And still, you're both here to make it right."

"Auntie, she's involved with someone else now. I just bring up bad memories for her now."

"Stop talking like that! What did I just say about negative talk? What God brings together, let no man put asunder. Have you signed any papers? Has she filed any?" His aunt asked.

"No."

"Then it isn't over. After you get settled, take the car and go see Jazmin. Surprise her with flowers and that charming smile of yours."

"I will. Has anyone heard from Derek?"

"Derek is on house arrest. They were saying on the news that the jury should start deliberations by the end of the week. Ask me, it ain't lookin' good for him."

"I wanna go see him before I leave." Shawne said.

After Shawne freshened up, he went to a floral shop, got a dozen yellow roses and a card, then headed to Jazmin's office. He parked across the street and walked towards the front door. As he neared the door, Jazmin and Stephon appeared from around the corner, holding coffee cups and laughing.

"Shawne." Jazmin said, caught off guard.

"Hey Jaz." He replied, holding the flowers and card.

There was a long awkward silence before Stephon broke it.

"Hey Jaz, I'll just call you later."

"No. I shouldn't have shown up unannounced. I'll leave." Shawne said, turning back towards the car.

Taking Stephon by the hand, Jazmin spoke to him. "Steph, I'll call you."

He agrees and kisses her on the cheek.

"Shawne!" Jazmin calls out to him as he gets in the car.

He watches her wait for traffic to slow down to cross, but he pulls off into the traffic at the first opportunity he gets.

Shawne drove around for hours. Surprisingly, he was not angry or upset. He was hurt. Hurting because it was sinking in that he caused all the pain to himself and most of the people around him that he loves. Despite what Coach Brown and Aunt Sheryl told him, that he still could make things right with his wife, he didn't feel it. He believed he had caused far too much damage.

Jazmin called him. He answered. "Hey Jazzy?" He said in a low sweet voice.

"You mean *Hey CoCo-Pop.*" Kayla said, imitating him.

"Hey Baby."

"Are you still here?" She asked her daddy.

"Of course I am. You are still leaving with me on Friday."

"Can you come over for dinner tonight? I'm cooking."

You're cooking? What are you cooking?"

"Spaghetti."

Shawne laughed. "You know how to make spaghetti?"

"O's. Spaghetti-O's" Kayla replied giggling.

"Gimme about two hours and I'll be there. I love you."

"K. Love you too." She said and hung up.

Shawne drove to the old neighborhood, and went to Derek's grandmother's apartment. He knocked and Derek opened the door.

"The hell you doin here? Slummin? He turned and walked back inside. Shawne followed.

"Bro, what happened to us? We always said nothin' would ever come between us. Money. Women. Fame. Nothin'. We shouldn't be like this." Shawne said.

"Yet here we are." Derek answered bitterly.

"D, I know you think I'm the cause of your issues, but I'm not Bro."

Derek sat there in silence, breathing deeply and upset.

"I can't make you talk to me. I just wanted you to know I got you in prayer and apologize to you for what's become of us. Peace, Kid." Shawne said, heading to the door.

"I know you had nothin to do with my case. I knew that all along for real. It's my own fault I'm here. I got the big head, thinkin' I was invincible. Straight trippin'. I know why you had to distance yourself from me."

"Dude, I didn't want to, but as you can see, I had my own drama I was dealin' with."

"Yeah, my bad on that too. I shouldn't have told Jaz. I was so pissed off! Crystal gone. DJ." Derek looked up at Shawne with fear in his eyes. "Nigga, I know they finna give me an L. Life."

"You couldn't cop a plea?" Shawne asked.

"Yeah. Turn state's witness against Lock and Con, for a 20 year bid. Shiiid. I'd be dead in 20 days in County if I did that."

"D, I don't know what to say Bro."

"You said enough just to see me. By makin' sure we good. You made me become the man I was. I lost my way on my own, but I owe the world to you. I saved every penny of DSE. There's a nice piece of change in that account. Make sure my son, niece, and now my nephew as well are set up for life. You were always the secondary account holder, Not Crystal or Jazmin. Who put this thing together? We, that's who." Derek mimicked Scarface.

Shawne smiled, recalling the countless times Derek would imitate people.

"I love you D. I got you" Shawne assured him.

They hugged for what seemed like an eternity. They talked a while longer before Shawne headed to dinner with Kayla and Jazmin.

He rang the doorbell. Kayla answered the door.

"Don't you live here too? Why are you ringing the bell?"

"Just let me in, Doodlebug." Shawne said, picking her up and tickling her. She giggled. As spun her in the air, he turned and Jazmin was standing there. Shawne suddenly stopped and put his daughter down.

"Kayla Baby, run up and take a bath before dinner. Let me talk to Daddy." Jaz said.

Kayla looked at her father. He nodded that he would be ok and she ran upstairs.

"No matter what, that little girl will forever be in your corner." Jaz complemented.

"What's up?" Shawne said as he stepped into the livingroom.

"Shawne, sit down please." He sat. "Let me get right to the point. You caught me off guard today showing up like you did. But more so when you didn't trip on me or Steph when you saw us."

"You really don't know why?" Shawne asked.

"Wait. Let me get this all out. Stephon really felt bad about how he treated me when I decided to break things off with him. He was hurt because I wanted my marriage to work out. He was trying to be everything for me that you wouldn't. And when I thought about it, I mean really reflected on the times I spent with him, they were great times. He made me smile."

"Jaz, I can't fault you for movin' on. I lied to you, I cheated on you. Had a child with another woman. I told you she was my true love. Simple truth is, I was greedy. I wanted you both for as long as I could get away with it, and ended up losin' you both. But I'm learnin' from my faults. I'm trustin' God to guide me daily. It hurt to see you with him today, and happy. But you deserve all the joy life has to offer. So I can only respect your wishes and know that I'll support you. But also know..." Shawne takes her by the hand. "Know how truly apologetic I am for all I did to hurt you. To undermine you for being the great mother and wife you are. I just hope one day you can accept my apology, and some good can come from it."

Jazmin was in awe and almost brought to tears by Shawne's words, his growth and what seemed like maturity. Kayla ran back down, jumped in her daddy's arms, looked at her mommy and asked. "Is it time to eat?"

Chapter 12

Legacy

Shawne and Kayla pulled up to the location where everyone was gathering for Coach Brown's Repass. "Daddy, was that man your grandpa?" Kayla asked

"No Baby. He was my high school football coach. A mentor."

"What's a mentor?"

"Like a father figure. He was that for me and a lot of others." Shawne said.

"So are you my mentor?" Kayla asked.

"I'm your father. But yes, I will always be here to guide you in the right direction. Like my dad did for me. Coach Brown was an exceptional man. He touched the lives of everyone around him. Let's go inside and see what's to eat." Shawne suggested. Kayla agreed.

Inside, Shawne looked around as Kayla tapped his hand. "Daddy. Is that your friend over there?" She asked, pointing across the room.

Shawne looked that way, and saw Roman. They walked towards him. Roman stood and met them halfway.

"What's up Cali?" Roman said, before bending to place his hands on his knees to speak with Kayla. "Hey there Lil' Bit. Do you remember me?"

Kayla smiled and nodded. "You're my daddy's friend."

"I am. Do you remember my name?"

"Umm... Umm..." She then shook her head.

"That's Uncle Ro, Kay-Kay." Shawne said.

Roman looked up at Shawne and smiled. "Yup. I'm your Uncle Ro. And the last time I saw you, you were this little."

"I'm almost eight now, and I play basketball. Do they have vegetables here? I still have to grow more." Roman laughed. "Yes they do. Grab your dad's hand and let's get you some vegetables."

They sat at the table to eat, Shawne turned to Roman. "Ro."

"Don't say it. As always Bro, we're bigger than the little things. Just do me one favor."

"What?" Shawne asked.

"Complete the legacy. Get my nephew." Roman said.

Shawne nodded.

"I bet you look just like your mommy." Ro said to Kayla.

"Nope I look like my daddy."

"Are you sure?"

"Yup. Every time I get in trouble, she says *Kayla Monae! Get over here! Lookin' like you're Daddy!*" Kayla said, attempting to sound like her mother yelling. Everyone in earshot laughed.

"I can't believe he's gone. It still feels like yesterday, hearing him call out a play from the sideline or yellin' at one of us in practice for a busted play." Roman recalled.

Shawne smiled. "Yeah. I remember the first time he called me in his office askin' if I had issues with Travis. That was the only time I ever lied to that man. I learned real quick, the worst thing you could ever do is lie to Coach Brown."

A few other former players that came to pay respects gathered with Shawne, Roman and Kayla to share stories about the great Coach Winston Brown.

A day later, Shawne and Kayla flew out to Atlanta. As they walked through the terminal, the television monitors caught Shawne's attention. Reports were coming in that Cory Tyson, Dante Ford and Derek Johnson were found guilty on all charges.

"Damn D." He mumbled under his breath.

Shawne texted Tasha letting her know he and Kayla were in town. They decided to meet at a park near the hotel. Tasha arrived holding Lil Shawne's hand. Although she was still very beautiful, she looked extremely tired and exhausted to Shawne.

"Hello Pretty Lady. What's your name?" Tasha asked Kayla.

"I'm Kayla." She replied.

"I'm your daddy's friend, Tasha and this is your little brother Ta'Shawne."

"You mean my daddy's girlfriend right?" Kayla said. Shawne firmly, yet gently squeezed her hand for a second. "Ouchy Daddy."

Shawne knelt down to one knee. "Hey Lil Man." Shawne said, holding his arms out.

He held tightly to his mommy's leg. "It's okay Shawny. You can go to your Daddy."

"Shawny? Are you serious Tasha?" Shawne asked.

Kayla walked over to her little brother and took him by his hand.

"Come on Lil Bruh Bruh. Let's go play on the swings." He let go and went with Kayla like he's known her all his life.

Shawne and Tasha sat on the bench and began to converse.

"I'm glad you reached out Shawne. I was ready to give up, but Mommy always believed you would come around."

"Did she? I love that lady like my own mother. I can hear her responding if she heard me say that. *I am Mommy.*" They both laughed.

"You've always been her favorite. Now she dotes on Shawny... Lil Shawne, just like she would you."

"Tash, I'm sorry I've been absent in his life up to this point. But that's over now. I struggled with the idea of just co-parenting with you and us not being together. But I'm puttin' my priorities in order. God first. Then those two over there." Shawne professed.

Tasha watched him as he stared at his kids playing together. "So are you divorced now?" She asked.

"No. But she has moved on." Shawne replied, lowering his head.

"You still love her?"

Shawne looked up at Tasha.

"Shawne, it's ok. You can be honest with me."

"I do." Shawne answered.

Tasha smiled, but hurtfully. "Then hold on. If it were over for her, you'd already have those papers." She rubbed on his back.

"If it's meant right?" He asked.

"You know better than anyone I know. So look, I have a doctor's appointment to get to. I trust you to take care of your son for a few hours. If you have any problems, I'm sure Kayla can handle it. I'll text you my address for you to bring him home."

"Appointment? Is everything ok?"

"Just a regular checkup. I'm fine. Let me slip away before he notices."

"Okay. See you in a bit."

After Tasha left, Shawne went and began playing with the kids. Lil Shawne was having so much fun, he forgot his mommy was ever there.

"Daddy?"

"Yes KayKay?"

"Lil' Shawne wants ice cream. Right Shawny, you want ice cream." Kayla convinced her brother. He responded by nodding his head.

"Oh yeah? What flavor does he like?"

Kayla looked at him. "Umm, he likes cookies and cream."

Shawne shook his head. "Aiight. My kids want ice cream, my kids get…"

"Ice cream!" Kayla yells. "Ice ceem!" Lil Shawne mimicked.

Later, when Shawne pulled up to Tasha's house, both the kids were fast asleep in the back seat. He texted Tasha to come outside instead of waking both up. Ms. Keyes came out with her daughter. She hugged Shawne with the same love she has always had for him, and adored his beautiful little girl as she slept. Tasha scooped her son up.

"Tash, can I talk to you for a second?" Shawne asked.

Tasha handed Ta'Shawne to his grandmother. "What's up?" She asked, watching her mother walk towards the front door.

"Thank you for today. Having both of them today, watching them get along like they've always had each other, really ignited somethin' in me. Tash, again, I'm sorry, and I know I can never get that time back. But I'm here now. Here." He hands her a check for fifteen thousand dollars.

Tasha looks at the check. "Shawne, you know it isn't about the money…"

"I know. It's about puttin' in the time, and playin my role in his life. I got it. I got him." Shawne finished her thought. She hugged him.

"Thank you." She said in a crackling voice.

He kissed her forehead, and walked to the driver's side. Tasha, with tears welling up in her eyes, she watched him back out the driveway. She wanted to stop him and share with him the issues she was dealing with, but she didn't. Tasha knew Shawne would try to move mountains to make things right for her. It would crush him to know he couldn't.

Chapter 13

Days Of Our Lives

Over the next several months Shawne was in a very peaceful and content place in his life. He spoke with his kids daily. He and Roman are on good terms again. He has found a church home in the Houston area. He Tiffany and Aunt Sheryl communicate weekly, as well as having a writing correspondence with Derek, who was sentenced to twenty years for his role in the murder of Ebonii Wells. Some very prominent influences spoke on his behalf, saving him from the life sentence he was facing.

As far as the women in his life, Jazmin was short but cordial with him. He could feel the distance growing more and more between them. And with Tasha, communication was good, but he could sense something was not right with her. Tasha called him late one night.

"Hello?" He answered his phone.

"You sleep Big Head?"

"Naw. How are you?" He asked.

She took a few deep breaths, then coughed. "Fighting a bit of a cold, but I'm good."

"Tasha what's up? Things don't seem right with you."

She stayed silent for a long moment. "Do you remember the first night we talked on the phone?"

"Until the next morning. You kept asking me if I was sleepy and ready to get off the phone."

"And you would say, *I'm sleepy, but I'm not sleep.* I recall that day like it was yesterday." Tasha added with a smile.

"I recall every moment with you like it was yesterday Tash."

Tasha, laying across her bed, stares at the ceiling, fighting back tears. "I like watching you play pro ball, but I loved watching you in high school. You had a yearning for the game back then. Now, you play…"

"Like it's a job. I didn't miss it one bit last season when I was hurt." Shawne interjected.

"Do me a favor Shawne? Find that love again, before it's too late. What seems like yesterday, is here today and gone tomorrow."

"And tomorrow isn't promised." Shawne added.

"Right. Life is short Shawne. There's so much to do, in such little time. Are you still coming next week?"

"I'll be there Monday. Flying straight there from Jacksonville."

"Okay, well I'll let you get your rest."

"Wait Tash. Tell me please. Is everything alright with you?"

Tasha removed the phone from her ear, breathed deeply, attempting to compose herself as best she could before answering.

"As good as things can be, Shawne. I'll always love you Shawne Thomas." She spoke in a low soothing tone.

"I love you too, Tasha Keyes. Good night." He said, trying to sound strong.

In LA, Jazmin and Crystal are hanging out talking. They haven't spent much time together outside of work since Derek's trial.

"Crys, talk to me girl. You've been quiet for months. Stop holding it all in."

"What do I say? I feel played. I let my guard down and Derek played me. I should have followed my first instinct years ago and left his ass right there at that bench in front of the arcade. Now I have to raise my son on my own."

"Don't I know it. Going through the same thing. They both showed so much promise in the beginning." Jaz stated.

"Yeah. Now one is in prison and the other is on the other side of the country with a whole new family. Speaking of which, what are you waiting for to send divorce papers?" Crystal asked. Jazmin hunched her shoulders.

"Jaz. You know. Tell me."

"When I started to tell Shawne how Steph and I started back up, he didn't wanna hear it."

"He got pissed off again?" Crystal asked.

"No, that's just it. It's like he gave me his blessings to move on. And since then, he has been very respectful of my space and time." Jazmin explained.

"Cause he's out there laying up with the homewrecker."

Jaz shook her head. "Nope. He isn't with her either."

"I be damn Jaz. You still love him."

"He's the father of my child. Of course I do."

"Trust me, that means nothing. You're afraid of losing him. That's why you haven't divorced him. Does Stephon know where he stands with you?" Crystal asked.

Jazmin looks at her friend, without replying.

Early Sunday morning, Shawne was awakened by the ringing of his cell phone, as he slept peacefully in his Jacksonville hotel room prior to that afternoon's game.

"Hello?" He spoke in a low tone.

"Shawne?" The weeping sorrowful voice of Ms. Keyes spoke.

Shawne knew something was wrong immediately. "Ma? What's wrong?"

"My baby. My baby girl is gone!" She wept.

Shawne sat up, shocked and amazed at what he just heard. "Wait... What? Tasha's what? Ma, how? What happened?"

Ms. Keyes tried to compose herself as she explained. Shawne, she has been very sick. Some type of respiratory disease for over a year now."

"I'm on my way." Shawne said urgently.

Shawne informed his coaches about the tragedy, and caught the first flight to Atlanta. When he got to the house, Ms. Keyes opened the door and embraced him so tightly. She began crying again. "I'm here now Ma. We'll get through this together."

After he closed the door, Lil Shawne saw him and ran to him, jumping into his arms. "Hey Man!" He said holding his son, as emotions began to overtake him. "Have you spoken to Ro and Erica yet?" He asked Ms. Keyes.

She nodded. "They will be here soon. Shawne, sit down please. I need to talk to you. You know, God moves in mysterious ways. I can count three different incidents that Tasha should not have been here in the last 14 months. But she held on for one reason, and one reason only. For you."

Shawne looked up at her. "Ma, Tasha made it clear a while ago, she and I were finished. I accepted it."

"No. For you to be in your son's life. To raise and train him up. I believe once she knew you were ready to take that responsibility, there was no need for her to continue suffering. Shawne, I tell you all the time. You are my son. And Tasha, well, no one would ever measure up to you. She loved you more than anything in this world, until that little rascal came along. He is so precious. But I can't raise him to be a man. Only his father can."

Shawne was deeply overwhelmed. With the praises, the responsibility that now sat in his lap, and this tragic loss that now leaves his son without a mother. Shawne knew some huge decisions would have to be made, and fast.

That night, he laid in Tasha's bed, with Ta'Shawne next to him, sound asleep.

As his eyes got heavier, he turned his head into the pillow and caught a whiff of Tasha's fragrance. He got weak and began to cry. "Tasha, Baby, why didn't you tell me sooner? Why?" He weeped over and over. Until he fell into a deep sleep.

"Shawne, you wouldn't have been able to fix this one, and I knew you wouldn't accept my fate."

"Tasha? He asked, sitting up in bed.

"I knew I was sick. I knew when I told you we couldn't be together again. I knew you would struggle with that because finally, you chose me. You chose us. But I also knew that it was not the path God called for us. Shawne, I need you to raise your son, our son in a strong family atmosphere. He has a father and a sister. Go get your wife back."

"Tash, this is easier said than done. This is too much at once."

"I prayed to God when I first got sick, begging for a miracle because I thought only I could care for my baby. But He kept showing me that I can only go so far. I kept fighting and fighting. Then you called and you showed up. God showed me over and over that you would show up. Shawne, when times were the hardest, I never knew anyone who stepped up bigger than you. I began to trust that you would do what I thought only I could do. I know this is alot, but you will find a way. It'll take sacrifice, but you can handle it." As Tasha spoke, Shawne could feel her getting closer to him.

He jumped out of his sleep. He wiped his eyes and looked around, then down at his son. "I love you Tash." He said, rubbing Ta'Shawne's head. I love you too Tash." He said, looking out towards the moonlight peering through the window.

At the repass, Shawne was comforted by friends and teammates. Both current and former. Including Roman, Bo, and Travis.

"What's your gameplan Cali?" Roman asked.

Shawne looked at him and kinda just slowly shook his head. He sighed deeply and responded. "Man, this is all new for me, and it's all hitting me at once."

"You thought of maybe hiring a Nanny? Like one that is flexible to travel with you. That way you don't miss out on Lil Man growing up." Bo suggested.

"I don't know if that'll work, Bo. I mean, would it be me raisin' him if I'm flyin' him all over the place with a nanny?"

Travis looked at Shawne. "Shawne? Do you still love the game? Like how you once did?"

Shawne fixed his mouth to quickly reply, but caught himself.

"Don't answer that right now. Just be truthful to yourself when you do." Travis continued.

"Me and Erica will always have your back Bro. Whatever we need to do." Ro told his friend.

Just then, Shawne's phone rang. He excused himself and walked outside. "Hey." He answered.

"Hey. Are you in town? Kayla keeps asking for you."

Shawne huffed. "Dang! I was supposed to come and spend time with her. I had to come to Atlanta. Tasha…"

"It's fine Shawne. I guess y'all gonna work things out." Jazmin interrupted.

"No. We haven't been together since before 9/11. I'm here now for the funeral." Shawne calmly stated.

"Oh. I'm sorry. Who passed?"

"Jaz, lemme call you back later tonight. Tell KayKay Daddy loves her and I'll see y'all soon." Then he hung up.

Erica came outside, holding Ta'Shawne's hand. "You good Shawne?" She asked with concern. His eyes watered and he choked on his breaths.

"No. I'm not. How am I supposed to make this work?"

"Tasha was more than my best friend. She was me, I was her. Growing up, nothing or no one could ever come between us. We never fought, we never argued. No matter how wrong I was, She always backed me. And vice versa. Then the summer of '88 these two boys came along sweatin' us in the mall and the rest is history. We both fell head over heels in love with them. Nothin' has changed either Shawne. A piece of us was laid to rest today, but more of her lives within us than what has died. You know what it takes. You got what it takes." Erica said, placing his son's hand in his hand then hugging him.

"Love you Sis" He said.

"I love you too. Erica replied.

Chapter 14

Moving On, Again

That night Shawne called Jazmin back. She was very concerned as she awaited his call. She answered before the first ring finished.

"Shawne. What happened?"

Shawne took in a deep breath before answering, making sure he was composed.

"Tasha... She's gone."

Jazmin just held the phone. She couldn't find the words to say. She never liked Tasha for obvious reasons, but she'd never wish death on her. Finally, she responded. "My condolences to you, her family, and her son. You wanna talk about it?" She asked, so very endearing.

Shawne sat up, somewhat shocked by her question, but not at all surprised. He knew her heart underneath all the scarring he caused.

"The collapse of the towers caused her health issues."

"So you've known since then?" Jazmin asked.

"No. She only recently somewhat told me she was sick."

"Somewhat? What does that mean?"

"She told me, but she didn't tell me just how serious her condition was. But how important it was to her that I was here for Ta'Shawne, and..." He stopped himself, thinking of what Tasha said to him as far as getting Jaz back in his life.

"And what Shawne?" Jaz asked.

"And, makin' sure he and KayKay know each other."

"That is very important. They need to know each other." Jaz added.

"How are things with you and Arthur, Stephon?" Shawne sarcastically asked, lightheartedly.

"Shawne." She attempted to deflect.

"It's ok, Jaz. I can handle it. I think."

"Things are good. He treats me well."

"Good. You deserve it. I'm sorry I didn't." Shawne confessed.

"Didn't what? Treat me well?"

Shawne remained silent.

"Shawne, I felt disrespected, but never like you mistreated me. In hindsight, neither of us were ready to accept the responsibility of honoring the vows we took."

"No. You were ready. I wasn't. I broke the vow I promised before you and God. And I have paid for it dearly. I've confessed it to God and I'm tryin' to be a better person, day by day."

"I can see that. Do you regret marrying me?" As she asked him that question, the doorbell rang.

"Expectin' company?" Shawne asked.

"It must be Stephon. Can we talk later?"

"I hope so. Good night Jaz, and thank you." Shawne hung up.

Jaz looked at her phone, seeing he hung up. "Good night Shawne, you're welcome." She mumbled with a grin as she walked towards the front door.

Shawne and Ms. Keyes decided the best course of action would be for Ta'Shawne to go with Shawne now. As Shawne awaited the taxi to arrive to head to the airport, Ms. Keyes sat beside him on the couch, holding and looking at a picture.

She sighed deeply, holding back tears. "I always thought this day would be the starting point of what the future held for you two." She said, handing the picture to Shawne and sitting her grandson on her lap.

Shawne looked at the picture of himself and Tasha on the day of her prom. In the picture, Shawne was caught staring helplessly at her while she smiled beautifully for the camera. "I know exactly what I was thinking at that very moment." Shawne recalled.

"That you were holding the hand of the prettiest girl in school." Ms. Keyes replied, twirling at Ta'Shawne's curly hair.

"Definitely." He added, staring at him, stare into Tasha's beautiful hazel eyes that day, so many years ago.

Ms. Keyes stressed to Shawne just how much she loved him, that even a son born of her womb couldn't be closer to her. As the cab pulled up, they embraced. Shawne promised she wouldn't want for anything. That all of her bills would be handled. She kissed his cheek, hugged and kissed her grandbaby, then watched them drive away.

Shawne and his son flew out to Los Angeles so Aunt Sheryl and Tiffany could finally meet and spend time with Ta'Shawne. He also needed to speak with his new agent, Trace Cutler of Cream Sports Management, CSM for short. Trace was overly arrogant. He managed a third of the top paid athletes in the three major sports. Shawne barely spoke with him one on one the way he did with Derek. And that 6% fee wasn't making him feel any closer to him.

At his aunt's house, Tiffany asked him the same thing everyone is asking. "What are you gonna do Shawne?"

"Imma go see my agent. I don't know." He said.

"Maybe you can take a leave of absence for a few weeks." Aunt Sheryl suggested.

"Mama, Shawne don't work for Blue Cross/Blue Shield. If he can't be there, they will replace him." Tiffany warned.

"I'll see what options I have when I get there."

Ta'Shawne was watching cartoons in the livingroom, when he got up and walked to the dining area where the adults were. He climbed up onto Tiffany's lap, and rested his head on her chest.

"He's such a sweet little boy." Aunt Sheryl adorned.

"This is TT's sweet little man now." Tiffany claimed, rubbing his soft curly head of hair.

"Baby, you spit both of them out. Kayla looks like you, but this one, is your twin and has the exact same mannerism you did as a kid." Aunt Sheryl said.

"Oh Lord! Another Shawne. What this world don't need!" Tiffany said.

"Ha. Ha. Ha. Since Tash is so comfortable with his aunties, Imma go see my agent. I'll see y'all later." Shawne kissed each of them on the forehead and left.

Shawne walked into the towering downtown skyscraper, and caught the elevator to the twenty-ninth floor. The first thing he saw was a beautiful mocha toned young lady sitting behind the receptionist's desk.

"Damn!" He thought to himself.

As he walked towards her, she looked up from her computer. "Hello? How can I help you? She asked, smiling. He instantly noticed her pearly white smile, and her full glossed lips. She had dark brown eyes and her hair laid almost to her shoulders in a doobie style. He quickly looked down at her well manicured fingers and saw no ring on her finger.

"Hi." He stops and clears his throat. "Excuse me." He blushes. She smiles back.

"Hello, again. I'm here to see Trace Cutler, my agent."

"And whom shall I tell him is here?" She asks as she picks up the phone.

"Shawne Thomas."

She kinda drops her head and raises her eyes in surprise. "Shawne Thomas? Thee Shawne Thomas?" She asks with sass.

"I'm him."

"Hmmm… Hi, Mr. Cutler, Shawne Thomas is here to see you."

"Be right out. Thank you Kimistry."

"Chemistry? That's cute and different. Your parents must've had some real good chemistry to make you."

"That was cute. Corny as hell, but cute. It's spelled K-I-M-I-S-T-R-Y. Kimistry Jones." She said.

"And what was that 'Hmm' for?" Shawne asked.

Kimistry coyly hunched her shoulders and smiled as she closed her eyes. Just then, Trace opened the door. "Shawne my man! What's up?" He shook his hand. "Hey my condolences for your loss." He said, clutching his heart. "Come inside, let's talk. Kimi, hold all my calls."

"Yes Sir." She replied.

As he and Shawne walked to his office, Shawne looked back at Kimistry. She was looking back at him when she got up and walked over to the copy machine. She observed and processed everything she needed to about him in a matter of seconds. *'Six-five, about 225lbs, size 13 shoe, wavy, faded haircut, caramel complexion, and could hang a suit!'* She thought to herself.

And Shawne too spoke again in his head. *'Damn! The body matches the look. Babygirl has a great future behind her!'* He gawked at her booty as she bent over to pick up papers she dropped.

"Help me help you Shawne. What's up Bro?"

"I'm at a crossroad Trace. I now have a 2 year old son that I need to care for full-time. That's gonna be near impossible tryin' to do from Houston. What options do I have? Possibly a trade?

Trace sat back in his plush leather chair, put his finger tips together and began to ponder. He turned in his chair and looked across the Los Angeles skyline.

"Here's the issue Shawne. I could look for a trade for you before the deadline, but your value is low. I understand you have had several life-altering events occur since your championship victory, but the fact remains, you haven't put up the numbers on the field. Let me talk to the organization and see if I can work out a trade." Trace says, spinning back towards Shawne.

"I prefer to be here in LA."

Trace looked at Shawne with a dead look. "They have Casey Jacobs and Taylor Lowe. You'd be lucky to be third string here."

"I've outplayed Jacobs every time we went head to head. And who is Taylor Lowe?" Shawne defended.

"But what have you done lately? Fine. I'll make some calls and be in touch with you." Trace said standing up and extending his hand to shake Shawne's. Shawne slowly rose to his feet, and shook Trace's hand, but he did not feel confident with this meeting.

"Tell you what. Set an appointment with Kimistry to be back here on Friday. She will check for an open time slot."

"Aiight." Shawne replied, then walked out.

"He wants you to set an appointment on Friday for me."

Kimistry looks at the calendar. "How does 10am sound?" She asked.

" How does 7:30pm Friday sound? Dinner. Me and you?" Shawne flirts, writing his number on the back of a business card.

Kimistry smiles. "Make it 8pm and I'll consider it."

"8pm it is. Call me." Shawne said, as he slowly walked backwards towards the door.

"Consider it considered. You'll be getting a call." She replied.

Shawne smiled, winked at her, turned and walked out the door.

Chapter 15

Shiesty Ish!

Sunday dinner at Aunt Sheryl's was normal. Jazmin, her mom, Crystal and the kids decided to join Shawne's family this evening.

"Auntie, where's Daddy?" Kayla asked Tiffany.

"He's in Houston. He'll be here later this week."

"When did he go back?" Jazmin asked.

"Yesterday. Lil' Shawne is here." Aunt Sheryl added.

"Shawny?" Kayla hollered out.

"Huh?" He answered, as he came running towards her from the other room. They hugged.

"That's so sweet. Hey there Handsome." Crystal said, squatting down to greet him.

Jazmin looked awkwardly at her mother. Tiffany noticed.

"Doodlebug. Take your brother and cousin in the backyard and play." Tiffany said to Kayla.

"Okay. Come on y'all."

"Let's sit. We got about forty minutes before dinner will be ready." Tiff continued.

They all sat, and the tension in the air was very noticeable.

"How have you been Anita?" Aunt Sheryl asked.

"Hold on Mama. We all family here. No need for small talk. Jaz… Speak your mind Sistah." Tiffany directed.

Jazmin repositioned herself on the couch, and cleared her throat.

"Ok. Since we are family, lemme ask all of you here this. How would you feel watching your child hug and love on their younger sibling that isn't your child because your husband had an affair?" Jazmin asked. The room was quiet before Crystal spoke up.

"Well, y'all already know my situation and what Derek has done. I may not have shown it, but I was hurt. He broke me, and I hate him with everything in me because of it. But there are times when I really miss him and I actually try to look at it from his point of view. Where did I go wrong to push him to the arms, to the bed of another woman?"

"Men are men. They're gonna do whatever they can get away with. It's just their nature. My soon to be ex-husband was always at work, allegedly, when in reality, he was drinking, gambling, doing drugs and hoeing all over the city. I had my intuitions about it for quite some time, but rather than bring it to him, I set myself up to move on, then served him at work to embarrass him and show him I wasn't playin". Tiffany surprisingly shared.

"Wow Tiff. I had no idea." Jazmin said.

"Baby, you know how I feel. Make your marriage work at all costs." Ms. Davis began. "I drove my husband to another woman with accusations that all turned out to be false. Shawne has made mistakes. I believe he's paid dearly for them and he is learning from them as well. But I also know, none of this is that baby's fault."

"I don't blame the baby Mommy. I just don't know if I'll feel right interacting with him." Jazmin defended.

"The blessing is in learning how to forgive no matter how much or how bad you've been hurt. The way God forgives us. We all have been through trials and tribulations with men. Mine, God rest his soul, passed on when Tiffany was three, but I had my fair share of rough times with him. Every story just shared just now are reasons why we are women. Because men can not handle the shit that they put us through. Excuse my language. I love my nephew dearly. As my own son. He knows I did not condone his actions, but the result, that little boy out there is a blessing. Spend time with him. That's Shawne incarnate. You will instantly fall in love with him." Aunt Sheryl said.

"Go out there Jazzy." Her mother insisted.

Jazmin was still a bit reluctant. It was just a discomforting feeling inside her. Then Tiffany got up. "Come on." She said to Jazmin, reaching her hand out.

Jazmin accepts her gesture and they go out back together.

"Who wants to play Duck Duck Goose?" Tiffany asked.

"That's for babies." Kayla said.

"Lil Shawne is a baby, KayKay." Tiffany replied, winking her eye at Kayla.

"Okay. I'll go first." Kayla stated.

They all sat in a circle. Kayla walked the outside of the circle, chanting, DUCK, DUCK, until she got to DJ and yelled GOOSE! DJ jumped up and chased Kayla around the circle twice, but didn't catch her. She sat where he was sitting. Ta'Shawne was so excited watching this. It seemed like he quickly picked up on the game.

DJ then walked the circle. He chanted three times around before Kayla yelled at him to pick. He touched Jazmin on the head and yelled GOOSE. She chased him around and around until he sat in her place. Jazmin caught her breath and began her chant. She called Goose on Ta'Shawne. He giggled, jumped up and chased her around laughing the whole time. When she finally sat down, he jumped in her arms excitedly yelling "I got you! I got you!"

Jazmin tumbled to her back, holding him smiling gleefully. "Yes Man. You got me." She naturally hugged him tightly. Unbeknownst to herself at the moment, that all the animosity, all the hang ups she held internally practically melted away with a simple game of Duck Duck Goose. Crystal Ms. Davis and Aunt Sheryl watched from inside.

"Congratulations. You have a grandson." Aunt Sheryl said to Ms. Davis. Anita smiled.

It's Thursday morning and Shawne's phone has been blowing up with calls and text messages. He opens his eyes, wipes them, stretches and yawns simultaneously. He picks up his phone to check what the messages say, before he could, his phone rang again. It was Bo.

"What's up Beef?" Shawne answered in a groggy voice.

"Obviously you're still asleep."

"Why, what happened?" Shawne asked, as he sat up.

"Thomas, turn to a sports network right now." Bo told him.

Shawne picked up the remote and turned his television on. And there he saw for himself. The headline of the morning. Shawne Thomas released!

"What the hell?!" Shawne blurted out.

"They said you asked for it."

"That's bull! I asked my agent about a trade because of my situation. Bo, lemme hit you back."

"Okay, bye." Bo replied.

Shawne immediately called his agent.

"CSM, Kimistry speaking. How may I direct your call?"

"Hey. It's Shawne. Is Trace in?"

"No Sir, Mr. Thomas. Mr. Culter won't be in the office today, but you are still scheduled to meet with him tomorrow at 10."

Shawne didn't know Kimistry well at all, but he could sense she was not being herself as she spoke to him. He paused a moment before speaking again. "Okay. Guess I'll see him tomorrow."

"Yes Sir." She said and hung up.

"Good job. Thank you Kim." Trace said as he walked back towards his office talking on his cell phone.

Shawne went to the facility to get clarity on exactly what occurred. He was in the office speaking with the general manager and the head coach.

"I understand the decision has been made and finalized. I'm just wondering what was said on my behalf, because the news reports are saying I demanded a release." Shawne began.

The GM and coach looked at one another, then the coach spoke. "Thomas, we know you have been dealing with alot, pretty much since you've been here."

"With the death of your child's mother, we thought at the least you would need some time away. Then Trace called me saying you wanted your contract restructured otherwise release you. We figured the latter would be best for both parties." The GM continued.

Shawne was shocked. He figured it all out right then. Trace wasn't making money off Shawne the way he was with other players, but he would get a nice profitable chunk out of a severance payment. He smirked slightly, sat back and took a deep breath. "I see more clearly now from your point of view. And I'm sorry I wasn't a better communicator about my needs. I did ask for a trade but money was never the issue. It was always about my family needs. But God has a plan. This will be a blessing." He thanked them for their time and went to clear out his locker. Shawne knew three things for certain. God was in control. His current representation was the sheisty grimey type, only paper chasing. And how badly he was missing Derek at this very moment.

The next day he flew home to LA and went straight to CSM. He was fifteen minutes early, so he waited downstairs before going up to see Kimistry. She texted him the day after he gave her his number. He replied, and they texted back and forth throughout the week. He texted her as he got onto the elevator.*'No matter what, we still on for tonite?'*

She quickly replied. *'Got my dress laid out on the bed already.'*

He grinned as he opened the door and saw her. Kimistry smiled lively when she saw him. Her first visual impressions of him were reconfirmed. The physical traits both Jazmin and Tasha fell head over heels in love with years prior. She continued her schoolgirl smile as she picked the phone to inform Mr. Cutler that Shawne had arrived.

"Send him in." Trace replied.

"You can go in." She stated.

"Can I?" He flirtatiously replied.

"No meet and greet at the door?" Shawne asked, as he tapped at the door then entered.

"Have a seat Shawne." Trace began.

Instead, Shawne walked over to the huge window and stared out. Then simply asked Trace, what happened.

I flew out there the day after we spoke. I had lunch with Billy, explained your situation and told him I had a trade deal set. Somewhere between my return here, words got crossed, leaks got out and they felt it was best to just sever all ties."

Shawne turned to Trace, then went and sat down. He stared at him until Trace looked away. "You know, I could really black out on you right now. But why? This is my fault. You see, my friend was my agent, and I picked up some things here and there being part owner of our company. Things like, the severance pay the agent gets upon a player's release. You never went to Houston. Let's not go any deeper into this. Are you gonna cut me loose from this agency right now with no further penalties? Or will we be seeing each other in court? I'm sure you know I'm also part owner of a very prestigious law firm not very far from here."

Trace stood up, walked over to his bar, and poured himself a drink. "Aww, what the hell. You're on the down side of your career anyways. I'll have the papers drawn up."

"Send them to my lawyer. I'll expect them within a week. I'll see myself out." Shawne said, getting up and leaving.

"I'll see you tonight." He said to Kim as he continued out the door.

Shawne went to Aunt Sheryl's, where Ta'Shawne has been for the last week. He has adjusted quite well to being around his grandaunt, whom he calls TeeTee and Tiffany, Tiffy.

When Shawne walked into the house, Lil Shawne ran top speed at him and into him like he was tackling him. Shawne played like he took a big hit from and fell to the floor, grabbing his son and hoisting him in the air, calling him the winner.

"What happened Baby?" His Aunt asked.

"I got screwed. Long story short, I got released, and I'm not with that agency anymore. I'm puttin' the condo in New York up for sale."

"So you're home for good?" Aunt Sheryl asked, smiling

"That's the plan. Hopefully I can get a tryout here, but if something else comes…"

"Here is where you need to be. Focus on that. Your family, your kids. Your wife." Aunt Sheryl interrupted.

"Auntie, I've hurt Jazmin too bad for her to consider any reconciliation."

"Oh, I doubt that. They came over for Sunday dinner. Kayla wanted to see her brother, and she wanted to meet him."

Shawne looked up in surprise. "She did? What did she say?"

"You will have to ask her that yourself. Kayla has a basketball game tomorrow. Wouldn't it be a wonderful gift for her to look into the stands and see her brother and daddy cheering her on?" His aunt asked. He seemed to agree, as he continued playing with his son.

At about 1pm, Shawne went by the law firm. Crystal was on her way out the door as he entered. "Hey Crys." He spoke

"Hey." She dryly replied.

"Look, I know alot has changed between us. I apologize for it all and just hope one day you can forgive me." He said, then began to walk down the hallway.

"Hey, you really should go see Derek. I think you would be surprised and shocked at some of the things you would learn." She said, holding the door open. Shawne stopped and turned back. "You've been to see him?"

"I did." Crystal answered with a smirk, recalling the ladies' conversation, then walked out the front door.

He knocked at Jazmin's office door. "Come in." She answered.

"Hey." He said to his estranged wife.

"Well hello there. What do I owe the pleasure?" Jazmin asked, smiling at the surprise visit.

Shawne smiled. "Stop. I stopped by to see if you wanted to grab lunch and to let you know to be expecting my release papers from CSM."

"Release papers? They let you go because of Houston?" Jaz inquired.

"No. I asked to be released free and clear after the stunt he pulled with Houston."

"I knew he was shady. You really need to do your own thing. You know the business."

"I don't know it well enough when it comes to that legal jargon."

"You got me." Jazmin quickly replied.

There was a long awkward silence between them as they locked eyes, almost fearing to be the one to look away.

"And lunch?" Shawne added.

"I, uhh... I."

Just then, a knock at the door and it opened. "Hey Babe, are you almost..."

"Steph. I was just..."

Shawne stood up. "Jaz, be on the lookout for those papers. I'll talk to you later. Excuse me." Shawne said, as he brushed past Stephon.

Stephon looked at Jazmin, crossing his arms and taking a huffing breath.

Later that evening, he pulled up to Kimistry's house. She walked out in a short black evening dress and heels. Shawne got out, hugged and complimented her. He then opened the car door for her to get in. Shawne walked around the back of his vehicle and looked inside. He was disappointed to see she did not reach over to open his door.

As they sat and ate dinner, Kimistry filled Shawne in on all the shiesty things Trace was up to. She told him she hated working there but it paid very well.

"Being someone else's secretary was your dream?"

"Hells no! I graduated with a degree in sports therapy."

"A masseuse?"

"It's more than being a masseuse. And I have a Master's degree thank you."

"Pro teams are always looking for good physical therapists. And I know it pays better than being Trace's secretary. How old are you, 25, 26?" Shawne asked.

"I turned 21 last month." Kimistry replied.

"Wha? Get the... You serious? Okay, gimme the rundown. Where are you from? School? Kids? Everything."

"I was born in Nashville, but raised in Dallas. I came here to go to school at Long Beach State. You know my major. No kids. And I rent my house with one of my line sisters."

"Lemme guess. You're a Delta." Shawne guessed.

"AKA." Kimistry corrected, holding her pinky up.

"Oh." Shawne said, a bit surprised.

"What?"

"I thought AKAs were light skinned. Your pretty brown tone puts me in a Delta mindset."

Kimistry laughed at his statement. "That's only in movies. Did you pledge?"

"Looking back, I probably should have, but I ain't wit all the hazin'. I wouldn't have crossed if one of the big brothers got crazy wit me."

"Again, too many movies Sir." She stated. Shawne hunched his shoulders.

"Tell me some things about you. Not involving football."

"Well, let's see. I have two kids. Kayla, 8, Ta'Shawne is almost 3. I was born in Jersey. Raised here and there, moving back here full time now."

"What if you get picked up by a team?"

"You said nothin' involvin' football. So I'm speakin' like I'll be here."

"You're right. I did. Continue please." She politely said.

"Yeah so, I'm back here, for the time being. I'm 29…"

"Are you married?"

"I am. But it's complicated." Shawne replied.

"How is marriage complicated? She says '*I do*' you say '*I do*', then you're supposed to live happily ever after."

"Well honestly, I did, she did. Then I didn't, and neither did she. Then my 'Didn't' had a son, and she moved on with her 'Didn't'."

"Damn. Drama. Why not just get a divorce?" Kimistry asked.

Shawne hunches his shoulders nonchalantly. "I don't know. I figure that will be her next move."

"Why haven't you filed?"

"It never crossed my mind to do it, truth be told."

They continued talking and enjoying one another's company, through dinner, and into a nice breezy walk along the Santa Monica pier. Kimistry felt a comforting chemistry with Shawne. She saw he wasn't trying to impress her with his celebrity status. When people recognized him and asked for an autograph, she saw how open he was, yet never brushing her to the side. She liked that. She had no issue with him being older, but she felt she needed to keep her feelings in control because of his marital status.

Shawne too was enjoying the evening in her presence. He was caught off guard by her age, and really didn't know how to think about it. But she was beautiful, so he figured, let the chips fall where they may.

He pulled up to her house and turned the car off.

"I really enjoyed this evening with you Shawne."

"Maybe we can do it again." He suggested.

"And again and again." She flirted.

They looked at one another before Shawne broke it, getting out of the car. He walked around to her door, opened it, and reached in to assist her out. Once she got out, Shawne could feel her grab a firmer grip to his hand, not letting go. He pulled Kimistry in close, taking a hold of her waist. He kissed her, and she reciprocated by gripping his shoulders, from underneath his armpits.

When they broke away, he hugged her.

"Do you wanna come inside for a little while?" Kimistry asked.

Shawne took a deep breath. He was so tempted.

"As good as that sounds, and I know what's on my mind… But I'm gonna pass this time. Let's keep it at this pace for now."

"Umm, ok. I like that." She replied with a smile.

Shawne walked her to the steps, and kissed her again. It was long and intense. So good, he had to pull away.

"You better go before it's morning."

"Yeah, and we sleep the night away." Shawne replied.

"I don't know how much sleep would be happening." Kimistry teased.

"Good night Pretty Woman."He said, peck kissing her one last time.

"Text when you make it home." She said, before turning to go inside.

After Shawne got settled at his aunt's house, he texted Kimistry, letting her know he was home. She sent him a picture of her lying in bed puckering her lips to the camera.

"Damn. Damn. Damn." Is all he could muster out.

Chapter 16

A New Game Plan

Shawne sat with Aunt Sheryl and Ta'Shawne a few rows up from Jazmin, Crystal, Lil D and Stephon, at Kayla's game. He watched his daughter play intensely, and he was very proud at how good of an athlete she was. At eight years old, he could see the fire in her eye for the game. Shawne noticed how every time Kayla would touch the ball, Stephon would get excited, then place his hand on the small of Jazmin's back and whisper in her ear.

"His sorry ass don't even know the game. Clappin' just to be clappin'." Shawne thought to himself.

After the game, Kayla ran into the stands straight to her father. She jumped into his lap excited about seeing him there.

"Did you see me out there Daddy?"

"Who? That little big headed girl all over the court, schoolin' the other little girls? Yeah I saw my CoCoPop."

"These girls are 9 and 10 years old." Kayla informed.

"Wow! For real? My baby ballin' like that?" Shawne says tickling her.

Kayla laughed, then hugged Aunt Sheryl.

"Gimme hi-five Shawny." She said to her little brother, as Jazmin and the others walked up towards them. Ta'Shawne began waving to Jazmin when he saw her face.

"Hey Shawny! Umm, little girl. Is your daddy the only person you see?" Jazmin asked her.

"Mommy, you brought me here this morning. I didn't know Daddy was coming."

"Great game Munchkin." Crystal said.

"Thank you Auntie." Kayla replied.

"Yeah, you looked really good out there Kayla. Hey Shawne, did you know those girls are older than Kayla?" Stephon asked Shawne, slowly grabbing a hold of Jazmin's hand, attempting to make small talk with Shawne. Shawne could see the insecurities Stephon had with him around. He observed the hand holding and smirked.

"Yeah. She told me. Her competitive genes run deep." Shawne replied sarcastically.

"Daddy can I stay with you tonight?"

"Of course you can, if Mommy says it's okay."

Kayla looks at Jaz, who in turn nods. Kayla gets excited.

"Can Lil D stay too?" Kayla asked.

"You wanna stay with us tonight Knucklehead?" Shawne asked DJ, grabbing him in a headlock.

DJ burst into laughter and asked his mother if he could stay with Uncle Shawne at Aunt Sheryl's house. She too agreed.

The kids stayed the night with Shawne. They watched movies, ate popcorn and candy. They pulled out sleeping bags and built a fortress in the familyroom with pillows and covers to sleep in. The next morning, Aunt Sheryl made breakfast and they went to church. Afterwards, Shawne took them to the park, went to McDonalds and then took the kids home.

After dropping DJ off, Shawne sat in the driveway to drop Kayla off.

"As always Daddy. Best time ever! But I have two questions for you." Kayla stated.

"What's up Baby?"

"Are you home for good?"

"Most likely, yes. Unless somethin' big happens." Shawne told her, trying to be as straightforward as he could.

Kayla looked around, at her brother, her father, and her mom came outside to meet her.

"What was your second question?" Shawne asked.

"Daddy, when are you coming back home? Here home. You and Shawny?"

That question sank deep in the pit of his stomach. All the wrong he's done. Hurting his wife, tearing his house apart. Yet, his baby girl could see nothing but her daddy being in her life, everyday. Being the ideal family that she's always wanted. Shawne closed his eyes, and before he could say a word, Kayla interjected.

"You're both here now, Daddy. Let's take it step by step." She kissed him on the cheek.

"I love you so much KayKay." Shawne said, choking on words.

"I love you too. Love you Shawny. See you later." Kayla said as she got out of the car.

"See you later." Lil Shawne replied in his little delightful tone. Jazmin waved as Shawne pulled out of the driveway.

Shawne thought alot about Derek since his return to LA. His issues with Trace and CSM, Crystal telling him to go see Derek, and Jaz hinting at representing himself, he felt compelled to go see Derek. It would be their first communication since his conviction.

Shawne sat at the glass window awaiting Derek to be brought out. Once he walked out, he sat, grinned widely at Shawne, and picked up the phone.

"My brotha! Damn it's good to see you Dude." Derek said, seeming in good spirits.

"How you holdin' up in here D?"

"I'm makin' it. Don't trip, but I feel more free than I ever have. Readin' alot, studyin' scriptures…"

"Scriptures? As in bible scriptures?" Shawne asked in surprise.

"Yeah bible scriptures. I was lost, but now I'm found."

"That's what's up D. I'm proud of you."

"Aye Shawne, I know you been through alot. I was supposed to always have your back through it all too. I'm sorry."

"We good Bro. You live, you learn." Shawne replied.

"Naw man. Your agent screwed you!"

"Ex-agent. I left."

"Yo. It's time to launch DSE. Change the name, whatever. It's time."

"What? The savings accounts you started for the kids?" Shawne asked.

"Shawne that wasn't a savings account Cuz. It's a legitimate bonded marketing agency. The plan was always to have something for our kids to own. That's still the plan, but with me stuck here, you need to keep it goin' Bro. You got ya first client already. Now you just need a few other things."

"What client? And what other things?"

"Shawne. You're the owner, and the client. Hire another agent or two, get a building to operate out of, and change the name."

"That all sounds well and good. I got money, but I'm not getting paid regularly right now.."

"Did I mention money?" Derek asked

"No. You didn't."

Derek looked around, then spoke in a lower tone. "Go to the office, look in the 3rd drawer on the left side of my desk. Inside, there's a book, on the inside cover, there's a card with a combination written on the back. Take down the picture on the wall, behind my desk, you'll see my safe. Open it with that combination, get the papers and go to the bank. They will be expecting you."

"Damn Derek. You was on some old mission impossible stuff, huh?"

"Cuz, I stacked like 4 million doin' this. Damn right I was on some mission impossible shit. And if anything would have ever happened to me, I had a plan. And if anything would have happened to me and you, I had a plan for that too. So there. I laid the blueprint. You set the game plan. Hopefully you keep me and mine involved."

Shawne became overwhelmed with what Derek just shared with him. With all they've been through. The ups and downs, and how he got upset with Derek about the whole DSE concept originally. He put his fist up against the glass.

"I got you D, always. Crystal and Lil' D too. That's my word."

Derek then placed his fist there. "Fa sho!"

After leaving the correctional facility, Shawne went straight to Derek's office. As he sat in his chair, and opened the drawer, Jazmin walked in.

"What are you doing?" She asked him.

"Oh hey. Come in and sit down. Do you remember the account Derek set up for the kids?"

"DSE? Of course. We still put something away in it each month. They got a little over eighty grand each." Jazmin replied.

Shawne continued step by step what Derek instructed. He turned around and dismounted the picture.

"Shawne, what are you doing?" She asked again. Then they both saw the safe.

"Apparently, Derek had bigger plans for the future. He stashed away about four million for the kids to one day start a sports marketing agency. Instead, he wants me to get it running now."

"So you're done playing?" Jaz asked him.

Shawne looked at the packet in his hand to take to the bank, then at Jazmin.

"Do you love him?" Shawne asked.

"Shawne, don't..."

"Jaz I know I messed up. I hurt you. Shattered your heart into a million pieces. And you may never trust me again. Jaz, do you love him?" Shawne asked with a pitiful look on his face.

Jazmin looked away, then at Shawne.

"Yes." She quietly replied.

The life seemed to drain out of him hearing that. Then his phone rang. Kimistry's name appeared on the screen. Shawne let it ring and then go to voicemail. She called back. Jazmin looked at it.

"Maybe you should get that. Kimistry really wants to talk to you."

Shawne answered. "Hey, lemme hit you back in like twenty minutes."

"Okay. You good?" Kimistry asked.

"I'm straight. I'll hit you right back." He disconnected the call.

"Who is Kimistry, Shawne?" Jaz asked. Shawne could sense jealousy in her tone.

"A woman I met a couple weeks ago. We went out once."

"Just once and now she's blowin' your phone up? Did you sleep with her?"

Shawne slowly closed his eyes and sighed.

"No Jaz. I wouldn't be askin you if you loved another man if I had someone."

"That didn't stop you in the past. You know what... I'm sorry. I shouldn't be doin' this with you."

"No. it's ok. I deserve it, and I'm not... I'm not gonna try to defend it. Like I said, I hurt you and you need to get it out."

Jazmin was taken aback by Shawne's response. The man she knew, married and loved would have been on the defense and hurled some type of sarcastic remarks back and they'd be in a shouting match. But this was a new Shawne. He seemed more open, more receptacle. Jaz liked the improved Shawne, she just wished his growth wasn't at the cost of her sake.

"Excuse me, I have a conference call in five minutes. Call your daughter later." Jazmin said, looking at her watch, then headed for the door.

Shawne watched her leave, then gathered the things he needed and left as well.

After speaking with advisors from the bank, Shawne learned that Derek had indeed built a strong foundation to start a sports management and marketing agency. In his mind, Shawne began strategizing. Two offices. One in New York. He could call some connections back East and see who would be interested in operating there. And the other in Los Angeles. Where he would run day to day operations. He decided to name it, Day One Sports. His focus, keep it all the way real with his clientele. To maximize not only the dollar, but the trust between agent and athlete. Shawne felt very confident with getting this venture up and running. He was ahead of the game, having played and connected with so many people. Now it was only a matter of networking.

He called Kimistry back after leaving the bank.

"Hey. Is everything okay?" She answered.

"Yeah. It's all good."

"You must have been around her when I called you."

"We were discussing some things but you weren't an interruption. I got some great news today."

"What's that?" Kimistry asked.

"Day One." Shawne said then paused.

"Come again? One day what?" Kimistry replied in confusion.

"Day One Sports. My own agency."

"Wow Shawne! That's great news. You makin' big moves real fast. Baller Baller!"

"Naw, nothin' like that. My boy made a really good investment for our kids' future, but we're gonna get this ball rollin' now. That's what took me so long to call you back. I had to get to the bank. Now I'm ready to celebrate, and lookin for someone to do it with me."

"I'm free after 6." She told him.

"Anywhere in particular?"

"Actually yes. I wanna cook for you. Then let's just kick on the couch and watch a movie."

"Hmmm… Dinner and a movie at Kimistry's. I'll bring the wine." Shawne said.

"I'll see about 6:30?"

"I'll be there at 6:28, Beautiful." Shawne declared.

After a delicious grilled chicken dinner, Shawne and Kimistry cuddled on her couch, to just the flickering light of the television. As she laid in between his legs, with her back to his chest, Kimistry began to play footsies with Shawne.

"I wonder what your massaging skills are like?" She questioned.

Shawne stuck his arms out to display his hands. "You see how big my hands are? I'm more than confident that my skills are better than yours."

"Man please! You know my skills pays the bills. You have no proof to back up your claim."

"Is that so? Okay." Shawne said, then placed his hands underneath Kimistry's shirt and with his thumbs began to massage her lower back in a slow deep circular motion, while his fingers held a firm grip to sides.

"Mmmm, ok…" She began.

"Shhhh. Don't talk. Just feel it." Shawne interrupted.

She leaned forward as he started moving up and down her back. Still slow deep circulating thumb motions, but now he included all his fingers, moving in wave like motion. Shawne moved up to her neck and shoulders. Gripping with his fingers and pressing with his palms. Softly but firmly squeezing and pressing, causing Kimistry to moan in great pleasure.

"Damn! I stand corrected." She confessed.

"You like that? You'll love this." Shawne slid his hands back down her back, and unhooked her bra. He leaned her back to lay on him and reach around front of her, cupping both breasts in his hands. Kimistry let out a relieving sigh.

"Close your eyes and slowly breathe deeply." Shawne said, whispering in her ear.

He caressed both at once, slow squeeze up, slow squishing motion down. Then both hands on one, massaging them in all different ways. Kimistry was in such a relaxed, satisfied state, that she had fallen into a trance. Shawne knew after this, his touch would be yearned for time and time again. He continued massaging her breasts until she snored. He then laid there until he too fell asleep.

Chapter 17

On Bended Knee

Several months have passed. Shawne officially announced his retirement from football at the end of the season. He is renting a loft downtown. He has Ta'shawne living with him regularly and Kayla is there quite often. She told her mom that her dad and little brother needed her to take care of them.

Shawne has found office space for Day One Sports (D1S) in LA but decided to postpone New York until he can better manage it. He speaks with Derek weekly, getting ideas on different moves to make.

He and Kimistry have continued spending time with one another, but still, at a very slow pace. They've discussed a committed relationship but it gets overshadowed by his complicated status with Jazmin.

Jazmin and Stephon have been going very well, until one day. As Jazmin laid in her bed, she looked to her left, the opposite side of the bedroom door. In the bed with her was Stephon, sleeping with his back to her. She heard a strange noise just outside the door. She tried to wake Stephon to see what it was, but he remained sound asleep. The door opened, and it was Shawne. He slowly walked towards the bed.

"What are you doing here?" She whispered to Shawne.

"You don't have to whisper. He won't wake up, he can't protect you. He can't because it's not his place to do so. You know, as well as I know all his insecurities. The sad thing is, he doesn't realize them. Always touchin' you when I'm around, like you'll run away. Yet he won't even sleep on the side of the bed closest to the door to protect you." Shawne continued as he sat on the bed next to her. Jaz sat up. Shawne stroked her hair, and caressed her face. Jazmine nestled her face into his touch, closing her eyes, feeling the comfort of being with her husband.

"Jaz, Baby he's a good guy. But he can never be me." Shawne leaned in to kiss her, and as Jazmin leaned towards him to receive his kiss... her alarm sounded off. She jumped up. It was daylight out, and no one was in her bed.

Stephon texted Jazmin a *'good morning'* text as he did every morning, and told her he made dinner reservations at a nice restaurant near the beach. Little did they know, Shawne made reservations for two at that same restaurant just moments prior.

The establishment was very elegant. Dimly lit, with soft mellow jazz playing. Jazmin and Stephon sat, sipping wine and talking as they awaited their meal.

"Jazzy, the times I've spent with you have been the best times of my life. Each day I wake up, knowing that I have you... It defies description." Stephon professed.

As he spoke, Jazmin looked up, and over Stephon's shoulder was Shawne. His date, Kimistry was being seated as he locked eyes with his wife. She inadvertently put Stephon on mute and began replaying her dream and the words Shawne spoke.

Shawne gave her a slight head nod and half a smile, as he sat in his chair.

"This is really nice Shawne." Kimistry complemented.

"I'm glad you like it." Shawne smiled, still glancing over her shoulder and Stephon's to look at Jazmin.

"What's on your mind? You said you wanted to talk to me about something." Kimistry mentioned.

"Relax Kimmy. We got all night."

"I got other plans for you all night. It's long overdue." She said to Shawne.

"Jaz? Jazmin my love, did you hear me? I asked you, have you given any further consideration to the divorce proceedings?"

"Stephon, I have." Jazmin replies.

"Great. Because I see a great future for us. We can sell both our homes and build. I never asked you this before, but do you want more kids?"

Jazmin took a sip from her glass, looked at Shawne, then back at Stephon.

"Actually I do. A son." Jazmin replied, weirdly thinking of Ta'Shawne.

Stephon smiled.

After dinner, Stephon ordered dessert for the two. Shawne and Kimistry finished and asked for the check.

"I'm gonna go to the restroom." Kimistry politely excused herself.

After she left, and the dessert trays arrived for Steph and Jaz, things got interesting.

"As I said Jaz, I love you and I'm willing to wait as long as I need to. Having said that, and always showing you how you deserve to be loved…" He lifted the top from the tray, picked up a ring box, and knelt down on one knee.

"Jazmin Davis, will you do me the honor of becoming my wife?"

Shawne saw this and slammed his fist to the table as he got up. Stephon and everyone in the restaurant became startled. He walked towards their table. Stephon stood up in front of Jazmin, and grabbed for her hand.

"Sh. Shawne?" He stuttered.

"It's Thomas. Jazmin Thomas. Arthur." He snarled at Stephon. He looked down at Jazmin. With hurt in his eyes and tone, he spoke.

"Congratulations."

Shawne turned and headed towards the door. Kimistry was not standing too far away when he took her by the hand and quietly left.

"What was that all about?" Kimistry asked, as they walked to the car. Shawne ignored her, as he attempted to collect his thoughts.

"Hello? Shawne." Kimistry asked, stopping in her tracks.

"Let's go for a walk." Shawne suggested. They got to the car, took their shoes and socks off and walked along the beach as the sun began to set.

"Kim, that was my wife and her boyfriend."

"Tell me what I don't know." She joked.

"He just proposed to her."

Kimistry turned and faced the ocean, squinting her eyes because of the sun.

"That must have hurt." She assumed.

Shawne looked into her eyes, past her beauty, right into her soul. He could see so many great qualities in Kimistry. He knew she was willing and ready to love him and only him. But he knew he would fall short of reciprocating that love to her.

"Babygirl, you have so much to offer to the right guy."

"So you're not the right guy?" She asked him.

"I have two kids, a deceased baby mama and a wife. I've only just recently begun to better control my temper and love myself the way God loves me. Creating another soul tie, having sex while I'm still connected to my wife is why I haven't been intimate with you."

Kimistry looked back at Shawne. She was confused on whether she should love him for trying to be an honorable man. Or hate him for feeling like she wasted her time on him these past few months.

"So what was this big surprise you had for me? You're breaking it off with me?" She asked.

Shawne took her by the hand. "No. But this was not the setting I planned either. I talked with some people and got you some connections with Dallas, New York and here. I told you before, you're better than just answering phones at CSM. All three of these organizations have top notch facilities. When I told them I experienced your work firsthand, they were eager to meet you."

Kimistry was speechless. She was extremely appreciative, but she had to ask again.

"Why now Shawne? Really is this your way of letting me go? Are you breaking up with me?"

"This was always the plan. To see you make it. Tonight was completely a surprise to us all. When I look at you, I see so much potential and promise. You will make a great wife and mother. And when I look in the mirror, I see how I failed two women that loved me unconditionally, but I was too selfish to love one the same. Kim, I've never filed for divorce because I still love my wife and want to fight for her."

"Shawne, you've been upfront and honest with me since the day we met. I'm willing to wait longer and continue at the pace we've been taking. I see your heart." She told him, as she held his hand tighter.

"No Baby. I can't ask you to put your life on hold and wait for me. Live your life."

Kimistry respected the man Shawne was. This version of him was all she knew. In her mind, she almost feared losing him. She figured there aren't many guys out there cut from this same cloth, but she knew she would have to let him go.

Shawne drove her home. They sat in the car, in silence for a bit before she spoke.

"Thank you Shawne."

"For what? You'll earn the job yourself."

"No thank you for everything. You showed me how to be loved without ever saying '*I love you*'. I'll set the appointments to be interviewed by each one of them. If it's here in LA, where does that leave me and you?"

Shawne looked into her eyes. He flashed back to that day years ago, standing on the pier with Tasha just moments before kissing her. He closed his eyes, then looked down.

"I gotta get her back." He spoke truthfully.

Kimistry, looking forward, closed her eyes as well. She then turned towards him, softly grabbed a hold of his head, behind his ears. Rubbing them, she pulled his head towards her, as she leaned in to kiss his forehead. She held her lips on him, while Shawne, eyes still closed, breathed in deeply. When she released the kiss, Kimistry whispered in his ear.

"I was at ninety percent." She kissed his lips, wiped a tear welling in her eye, and exited the vehicle.

Shawne got out after she did. "Kimistry." He called, but she continued towards her front door.

Shawne and Kimistry started a percentage count after almost a month together. He asked her if she was falling for him, and her first response was '*Yes. I'm at ten percent*'. The percentage continued to grow, so for him to hear ninety, he knew she was all in. But he also knew it couldn't go on. He watched her go into the house, as he still stood in the street.

Back at Jazmin's house, Stephon opened the front door, and let her in first.

"You've been awfully quiet. Not much conversation on the ride here, and I never got a definitive answer regarding my proposal to you." Stephon began, as he sat on the couch.

Jazmin sat down next to him. She happened to look at the mantle, at the wedding picture of herself and Shawne, and flashing back to slamming it to the floor during an argument they had. She bought a new frame and still, on the mantle, it sat.

Steph, do you remember the depths you sank to in order to get me to leave Shawne?"

"Baby, we've been over this. I was wrong. I was wrong for the words I spoke that day on the beach."

"No, I know you've apologized, and I've forgiven you. I asked because I wanted his dirt to be the reason I could walk away from him and start fresh. But I couldn't. Even when I found out that he was carrying on a whole relationship for years, and had a baby. I have yet to completely let this man go."

"What are you trying to say Jaz?" Stephon asked with concern.

"I'm saying… I can't accept your proposal at this time. It would only further complicate things in my life." Jazmin said, holding the engagement ring in her hand.

"Sweetheart, I've been here. I have shown you that I love you more than he could ever."

"Steph, I do love you. But love is not a race. Shawne, you, and myself. We've all made mistakes. I need time. Time alone. If I'm going to move on with you, I have to let him go. But at the same time, if I'm gonna make my marriage work, it has to be without you."

"Are you really breaking up with me right now?"

"Steph, I'm asking for space. If you love me like you say you do, let me go." Jazmin exclaimed.

Stephon stood up and walked to the window. He wiped the constant flow of tears streaming from his eyes as he stood there silently.

"Steph?" She called him once to no reply.

"Stephon, say something." She demanded.

"My everything revolves around you. And now I just have to let that all go? I'm afraid to lose you!"

Jazmin walked over to him and stood behind him. "Is that why you make it a habit to touch me or hold my hand when Shawne is around? You fear losing me?"

"I don't do that." Stephon defended, turning around.

"Nevertheless. I need time. Suffocating me right now, will surely lose me.

Stephon looked at her as she extended her hand to give him the ring back.

"Keep it. You are my wife to be. I know it. I'll see you in a month." He kissed her on the cheek and left.

Chapter 18

Building Foundations

Together, Shawne and Derek are vastly building their new empire. Two of Derek's former basketball players have signed on with Day One, and Shawne hired Harper on full time to do in depth background checks on every employee. He wanted no part of anyone that could potentially give the company a bad reputation. Shawne also hired another agent, Jackson Evers, a young, smooth, quick witted guy with a natural gift of gab. Shawne saw him as a version of Derek when he first got into the industry. Smart, savvy, and hungry. He had a promising pro basketball career that was cut short with a knee injury his rookie season. Shawne wanted to sign football players, but because he only has a bachelor's degree, he can't negotiate contracts directly for them. He goes to visit Derek to discuss the dilemma.

"It's gonna be hard gettin' football players."

"Why?" Derek asked Shawne.

"Negotiating." Shawne replies.

Derek laughed. "You do know I never had a Master's degree either right?

"But you worked out of the office with the ladies. They did."

"Ok. Then you know what to do Cuz."

"D, I'm still shocked Jaz and Crystal even speaks to me, and you think it's a good idea for me to ask them to unify the law firm and Day One so I can sign athletes?"

"Shawne it's business, Cuz. They gonna make money too. This is a win-win situation. And now you're back home for good, you can get things back on track." Derek stated.

"It's comin' around. We'll be in NYC in the near future."

"Naw Dogg. I'm talkin' about family. Gettin' your wife back."

"Why everybody puttin' it on me? Yeah, I missed up big time, but she's made her decision too." Shawne said coldly.

"Did she? You sure about that? Dude, you know Crystal is the hardest nut on earth to crack. Shawne that woman came to this penitentiary, I didn't ask her to neither. I figured she was all the way done wit me. Dude, she came, snapped on me, told me exactly how she felt, how bad I hurt her, and didn't hold back. Then she forgave me, and said *'this is the or worse part the pastor spoke of in our vows.'* Before she did that, I had been prayin', askin' God to soften her heart for when I found the guts to apologize to her. So for her to move first, when she did nothin' to deserve the way I treated her... Dude, I knew that was nothin' but God. From then on, I decided this imprisonment wouldn't consume me, I accept my role for what I did and why I'm here. Embracing my karma will make me be a better friend, father, husband, and man of God. I said all of that to simply say, Jazmin is so much more easygoing than Crystal. Pray on it, and accept your faults. If she don't make the first move, you'll see where she'll allow you to do so Bro."

Shawne listened intently to his friend. He could hear spiritual growth in Derek's words. After leaving, Shawne had Jazmin deep on the brain. He drove to the park where he and Jazmin as kids spent alot of time together. He recalled pushing her on the swing, as they talked and laughed. He then drove around the corner to where Crystal's mom still lived. Shawne parked the car, got out, and walked down to the corner. Standing there, he looked down the street at the tree where he first kissed Jazmin that Saturday in March back in '87. He walked down to it, touched it, closed his eyes and began to pray.

"Father God, thank You. Thank You for keeping me. For blessing me with all that I have. I thank You for never leaving or forsaking me. Lord, I stand by this tree right now, remembering one of the greatest gifts You gave me. Jazmin Davis. From the day I met her, each day she has gotten stronger, becoming the rock of our family. I failed her, Lord I failed You. Not honoring my vow, yet You kept me. And Jaz, I've constantly disappointed and deserted her somehow, someway. I've cheated, had a child with Tasha, and told her I chose Tasha over her. Yet she isn't completely gone from me. God I thank You for saving Derek. His rededication to You is an inspiration to me. Please Father, continue to bless these great men that live by Your word. Travis, Roman and Bo. They've made it their personal drive, their desire, to always be there for me. Showing me that You've never stopped loving me. Lord, I ask You to show me how to be the best version of me now. The best friend and family member I can be. The best business owner I can be. The best father to Kayla and Ta'Shawne. And the best husband to Jazmin. Yes! I speak it into existence! Jazmin is my wife! I will be the best and only husband to her! I speak these words to You, in the loving Name of Your Son, Jesus Christ... Amen." Shawne opened his eyes, removed his hand from the tree and wiped his eye. He walked back to his car with renewed confidence.

Several days later, Jackson walked into Shawne's office with some news.

"Shawne, Roman Goodman left a message for you while you were out." Jackson said.

Shawne looked a bit bewildered, while he pulled out his cell phone. "Why didn't he call or text me?"

"He said he would meet you at your Aunt Sheryl's house on Saturday." Jackson continued.

Shawne called Roman. It went to voicemail.

"He also said he can't talk to you about it before then."

Shawne wondered what this was all about. "What do you think this is about, Jack?"

Jackson shrugged his shoulders. "Not sure. The Draft is two months away. You think he may have a client for you to sign?"

Shawne continued to think. "I don't know. I'm still workin' on that dilemma though."

"Aiight well, I gotta run out. Got a meeting with a potential new client myself. I'll holla at you later."

"Aiight. Peace Bro."

After Jackson left, Shawne got a text. It was from Kimistry.

'Hi Shawne. I decided to text this rather than talk on the phone or see you face to face. Thank you for being the guy you are. Even though I could see myself spending the rest of my life with you because of your values, your willingness to provide and protect, I understand now why you did what you did. Funny thing is, it makes me want you even more (smile). I wanna tell you that I got offers, great offers from all three organizations. They all spoke so highly of you. You probably could still play and start for any of them too. I chose Dallas though. LA offered more, but being that close to you made it less for me. Shawne, thank you for showing me my worth. For treating as such as well. The next guy to come along will have some enormous shoes to fill. Take care of yourself, and get your family back! Yes, I have already moved into my new place here in Dallas, so don't go looking for me. LoL'

Shawne smiled, and texted back *'xoxo Luv U Girl! xoxo'*. Shawne knew Kimistry hated when people misspelled *'LOVE'*, so he did it just to tease her.

On Saturday morning, Shawne and Lil Shawne were on the way to the barber shop when he decided to call Jazmin. She didn't answer, so he left a message asking if they could talk later tonight or tomorrow. Roman was to be at Aunt Sheryl's around 7pm. As of 5pm, he hadn't yet heard back from Jazmin.

When Shawne opened the front door, he and Lil Shawne was startled by everyone in the house. "Surprise!!!" Everyone screamed in unison.

It seemed as though everyone from Shawne's life was there. His childhood friend, Brandon, old teammates, Roman, Erica, Tiffany, Ms. Davis, Crystal, her mom, DJ, as well as Harper, Travis, Bo, Kayla and Jazmin.

"Surprise? It's not either of our birthdays." Shawne smiled as he explained.

"So what Baby? We are all here to let you know that we love you." Aunt Sheryl said.

"Yeah. Even though you can be an ass, a pain in the ass, and a jackass… We all really do love you." Tiffany jokingly added.

"Thomas, not only got me a ring my first season in the league, but you brought me in the fold like I was a seasoned vet. That goes a long way with me." Bo said.

"Bro, you have made a difference in so many lives…" Ro begins before getting choked up on words. "And for the better part of the last twenty years, I've been right there with you. I've seen you deal with trials, tribulations, tragedies and triumphs. And no matter what, you always made it to the other side as a better man than before. You already know, not even blood could bring us closer, and I'm sure I speak for everyone else here when I speak these words. I love you Cali!"

"We love you Shawne!" They all yelled.

"But I speak for myself with this." Roman continued, as Erica handed him a folder. "With the help of your partner, Jackson, I am now represented by my best friend and his sports agency, Day 1 Sports!"

Everyone started clapping and celebrating the news.

"Wow! I was just thinking. What if Thomas represented me as my agent?" Bo said.

"My daddy should be everybody's agent. He's gonna be mine." Kayla said, hugging her father.

As everyone enjoyed the company of others, Shawne asked Jazmin to go out back with him to talk. She excused herself and followed him.

"Hey. Congratulations! Three new contracts tonight alone. That's big." Jazmin began.

Shawne grimaced as he thanked her. "Yeah, thanks. That's kinda what I wanna talk to you about. I mean, I don't know when I'll get another chance to speak with you before..." He stopped himself.

"What? Before what Shawne?"

"Jaz, I can't rep them without you and Crystal. I need you."Shawne stated, looking shameful.

"Is that all? You didn't know how to come to me and ask that?" Jazmin asked with a bewildered look. Shawne looked away, but Jazmin grabbed his hand, turning him back to her.

"Naw. I know you. What else? Talk to me." She demanded.

"I wanted to ask you about this partnership... Before, before you divorced me and moved on for good with your fiancee." Shawne struggled and choked on his words. He looked away again to keep Jazmin from seeing tears form. Jazmin softly smiled. She knew for the first time in a long time Shawne still truly cared. However, she was not yet ready to tell Shawne of her hiatus status with Stephon.

"Shawne, none of that should interfere with us doing business. Signing players benefits me just as much as it does you. Of course I'll assist in your Day One Sports endeavor. Crystal will too."

Shawne's whole face lit up hearing that. He held her hand tighter and looked her in the eyes.

"Thank you, Beautiful." He said, looking at her with intentions of kissing her.

Jazmin slowly stepped closer towards him, replying. "You're more than welcome." With a smile. As they drew nearer. Kayla and Lil Shawne ran outside, quickly forcing Shawne and Jaz to separate.

"Mommy! Mommy! Can my little brother spend the night? I need to teach him how to fight."

Jaz looked at Shawne, and the both kind of just smiled. Then Jazmin knelt down.

"You wanna spend the night with us?" Jaz asked Ta'Shawne. Holding his big sister's hand, he nodded.

"Okay." She pleasantly replied.

"Give Mommy a hug." Kayla insisted. He obliged.

"No one's gonna ask Daddy if it's okay?" Shawne asked.

Still hugging Jazmin, Lil Shawne turned back towards his dad. "It's ok Daddy."

They all laugh.

Chapter 19

The Comeback?

With things beginning to line up nicely in Shawne's life, he decided to take Lil Shawne to Atlanta to spend some time with his grandmother. While he was there, he took flowers out to Tasha's gravesite to sit quietly and reminisce on the past.

"Lil Shawne is doin' so well. He is growin' so fast too. I tell him about you all the time." He stops talking and stares at her tombstone. Shawne closes his eyes, sighs deeply, then goes to a knee. "You should still be here… Not me." After kneeling for a prolonged period of time, he got up and left the cemetery.

Shawne went by Roman and Erica's house to discuss business with his client and his upcoming free agency.

"You want anything to drink?" Erica offered.

"Bottled water if you have it, please." Shawne replied.

"Babe, you good?" Erica asked Roman.

"Yeah, I'm straight."

"Aiight so, what's up? You wanna stay here, go elsewhere, what? Because you know calls will start comin' in soon." Shawne began.

"I got one, maybe two good years left in me. I'm kinda torn." Roman stated, as Erica joined them at the table.

"What? Dude, you're barely 30 years old. I see 5 or 6 years left in the tank."

"Ha! You're not the one massaging his knees every night." Erica blurted out.

Roman sarcastically looked at his wife. "Naw Cali, I'll be 31 three days before you, and the last couple of years have really taken its toll on my body. You walked away under your own power. I may limp out, but not carried out. Two years max. Atlanta has become home, but New York or Tampa Bay would be considered as well."

"Baby. Tell him what else." Erica hinted.

"Tell me what?" Shawne inquired.

Roman smiled. "I'll sign a three year contract anywhere... As long as you are throwing me the ball again."

Shawne looked at Roman for a long moment. He saw that Ro was dead serious.

"You deadass?"

"As a heart attack."

"Roman. That wasn't what I was talking about." Erica cut in.

"Oh yeah... You finna be an uncle godfather in eight months." Roman proudly but nonchalantly added.

"Wha... But I thought."

"We tried in vitro and it worked!" Erica said, standing up to show Shawne her still flat belly.

"In V what?" Shawne asked, standing up to hug Erica.

"In vitro Bro. It's like a fertility process. Don't strain your brain. Just be happy and think about what I said."

"Congrats! I don't know a more deserving couple. And our family grows!" Shawne dapped and hugged his best friend.

"I know you miss the game Cali. And I know you got your new business venture rolling strong. That ain't goin' nowhere. Hell, the way I see it, Imma need a job in two or three years. I can broadcast or come work with you."

"Come work for me. I can use a big, speedy janitor." Shawne said, and the three laughed.

Upon returning home, Shawne couldn't stop thinking about Roman's offer. Returning to the field of play. It was true. He missed it alot. Shawne knew he had more in the tank and the way he retired, was not the way he wanted to end his career. He pondered on it. Then decided to speak with people within his circle. He spoke with Aunt Sheryl, who told him to follow his heart. She emphasized that no matter what, Ta'Shawne had a home with her. He spoke with Tiffany. She was not very fond of him returning if it would at all hinder their relationship again like it did when he was in New York. But she would support him otherwise. When he told Travis of the thought, he only asked him what he always asked him. Does he still love the game? If so, passionately, he too would fully support him.

Shawne went to his mother-in-law's house. Kayla was there visiting. He figured he could kill two birds with one stone. He sat them down.

"This conversation is between us three only. So let's keep it right here. We say exactly how we feel right here, right now. Ok?" He began. They both agreed.

"What do y'all think about me returning to play football?"

Ms. Davis' face drained slightly. "I thought you were happy with your agency?"

"I am. And that's not going anywhere. I just…"

"You miss it." She finished his sentence.

"I do." He hesitated.

"Honestly Shawne, I don't care for the thought of you returning. You are a much better person out of the league than in it. I'm speaking bluntly because I love you Son. But ultimately, it's your decision."

"I respect that Mom. CoCoPop?"

Kayla's face grew sad. "Remember you told me you wouldn't know where you would play? Is that still the same?"

Shawne's heart sank. He didn't want to lie to his daughter. "Yes Baby, I still wouldn't know."

"So… You would leave us again? And take my lil brother too?"

"KayKay baby, no I…"

Kayla stood up. "It's fine Daddy. Go play. I know you miss it. I know you only left to be there for Shawny. So go." Kayla turned and ran up to her room crying.

Shawne called out to her. "No. Let her have her moment." Anita said.

Shawne obliged. Kayla's bottled up anger cut Shawne deep to the core. Outwardly, she showed Shawne off as the perfect Daddy, but internally, she yearned for the father she needed in her life, everyday. That honest outburst put it all in perspective for him.

Shawne went to visit Derek. When Derek sat down, he had a look on his face like he already knew why Shawne was there.

"What?" Shawne blurted, as Derek just looked at him.

"I know why you're here. You wanna hear me say go for it Shawne. Don't do it Shawne. Which one?"

"The truth. How you really feel."

"The truth? Your truth? Or your family's truth? Because the truth is, no matter what you choose, someone gets hurt."

"Aiight, so what do I do?" Shawne asked.

"It's obvious you wanna return. You're an agent now. Act like one." Derek challenged.

"What you mean, act like one?"

"Aye Cuz, you buildin' an empire off the gift of gab. You already know what you want. Get it."

Shawne knew Derek was right. He already knew he wanted to return, and he knew what he wanted. Total control of the situation.

Shawne met up with Jazmin at her office. He was pretty certain she too already knew of his news. Her door was ajar, but he knocked anyway.

"You can come in." She said, still looking at her computer.

Shawne plopped down on the chair and just stared as Jaz continued to work.

"You can talk. I'm listening Shawne."

"Should I just assume you have heard my possible news?"

"Is that what it is now? News. Sounds like you have come to a decision. The way I've heard it, you are getting opinions. So you're here to break the news to me first? Because you never asked for my opinion." Jazmin asked, turning her attention to him.

"I haven't made a decision yet. Actually, I wanna tell you what I want."

"What do you want Shawne?" She asked.

"I hear the sarcasm Jaz. But I wanna make a comeback. I wanna play with Ro. But I don't ever want my kids to feel like they are without me. That I'm not around. I wanna continue my strive to be a better person. I want my family. And for them to know I'm here for them in every way."

"I wanna believe you with everything in me. And it's not that I don't. But I'd be lying if I didn't tell you that trusting you fully is just kinda hard for me still. Your being in the league tore us apart. You are so much a better person away from the field of play.."

"The league didn't tear us apart. I did that. It was my fault. I remember the night before the draft. You asked one favor of me. Not to change. But I did. And I see my faults clearly now, and never intend to make those mistakes again. That's with you as my wife or just as my friend. I came to you last because what you think matters most of all."

Jazmin watched Shawne intensely as he spoke, but tranced into a glimpse of the past. Her thoughts wandered back to March 7th 1987, against the tree where they first kissed. She blushed slightly, as she wiped a tear.

"Jazzy, you okay? Are you listening?" Shawne asked.

"I heard everything you said. If you can find the perfect situation and you are ready, physically, mentally, emotionally and spiritually… I'll support your decision."

"Really? No if ands or buts about it?" Shawne challenges.

"Fully. You know what you want and you know what's at stake. I'm gonna trust you."

Shawne was happy to hear her say that. He stood up and stretched his arms out to hug her, thanking her. Jazmin stood up, came from behind the desk and hugged her husband. He caught a whiff of the shampoo she uses on her hair and brought back great memories. The same effect happened on Jaz as she felt his strong grip around her, always feeling safe with him. Still holding her, Shawne stepped back to speak.

"Hey, can I take you out to dinner tonight?"

Jazmin awkwardly broke away from the embrace. "Uhh... I can't tonight. I'm going out with Stephon."

Shawne's heart sank, but he had to accept it. "I understand. Well, I'll let you know what happens before it hits the media. I'll talk to you later." He turned and headed out.

"Shawne." Jaz called out. But he just continued out the door.

That night Jazmin met Stephon at the marina. He planned a quiet romantic dinner on a boat. The time away from her was about a month and a half, but he did as she asked and gave her space.

Before they got on the boat, Jazmin wanted to talk.

"Let's talk first, Steph. I can't get on that boat beforehand."

"Ok. Let me go first then please. These past fifty-two days without you, have been hell for me. I couldn't help but to think you've been with him. But I know you haven't. I mean aside from helping him with his business and the one on one chat at his aunt's house. Oh and today at your office."

"Hold on. Have you been following me?"

"Well, no. More or less him. I gotta protect what's mine." Stephon declared.

Stephon then dropped to a knee. "So will you still?" He asked, taking her left and sliding the ring on her finger.

Jazmin slowly pulled away. "Stephon, I like you. I love you even. I asked you for space and you followed him around? Yet, whenever I mentioned you to him, it hurt him, but he allowed me to be me and do what I needed to do. He was right. Your insecurities would be our demise. In highsight, I see that now. I can't marry you, nor can I continue to see you anymore."

Stephon stood up and looked at Jazmin through glassy eyes. "You're breaking up with me?" He stepped towards her, as she backed up.

"Steph, this is what's best for both of us."

He grabbed her arms. "You're what's best for me! You can't break up with me!"

"She can and she did!" Crystal said, getting out of a car driven by Harper.

She walked towards them reaching in her purse. Stephon released her and stepped back.

"Crystal. Don't do something that'll have you as cellmates with your little thuggy husband." Stephon insulted.

Crystal pulled her cellphone out. "Oh this Nigga got jokes." She said to Jazmin. "You got jokes? Well let's play a game. Multiple choice. You get five seconds to pick one. A. You carry your weak ass over to that boat alone. B. I call the police for putting your hand on my girl. C. I call Shawne. You know he'll love hearing you grabbed on her again. Or D, my favorite. I yell over to that car and that back opens and one of my thuggy ass husband's associates gets out and handles all this." She raised her hand and the tinted back window rolled down.

"One… Two…"

"You blew it! He's done and washed up. Just another ex-athlete struggling to make it without fame. Fuck him, you and his bastard child!" Stephon yelled out.

"Five!" Crystal yelled out.

The backdoor of Harper's car opened and a man two times the size of the car stepped out. Stephon wanted no parts of him. He quickly turned and rushed to the boat, and sailed off.

"You ok Sis?" Crystal asked.

Jazmin nodded. "How did you know I was here and how did you pull all this off?"

"I walked into the office and overheard you and Shawne. After hearing what he said, I knew you would be hesitant about meeting with Stephon. And that you were breaking things off with him. Last time that happened, things didn't go so easy. So I called Harper and he was on it. We tailed you to make sure you would be okay, with his cowardly ass!" Crystal yelled out.

"Thank you." Jazmin said, hugging her best friend. "So Derek has a protection detail for you?" Jazmin asked, referring to the giant man from the back seat.

"Girl no. That's my cousin Big Rob from Long Beach. He's just big. Can't fight his way out of a wet paper bag." Crystal said, Jazmin laughed.

"I heard that Crystal." Big Rob said.

"So, And? Girl, go get your husband and family." Crystal said.

Chapter 20

Happily Ever After?

In the offseason, Shawne began a rigorous workout. Up six days a week at four in the morning to run three miles. Followed by a 1600 rep Push/Pull workout on alternate days. Then late mornings he would go through two hours of passing drills. Once he got to a point where he felt he could compete again, he and Roman began working out together.

Roman and Shawne sat down to discuss the next move. "Ro, I wanna do this, but I'm only willing with one team."

"New York, where you started." Roman replied.

"Naw Dude. LA."

"LA? They already have an All-Pro QB."

"He's not my concern. I gotta be here for my family. My kids. My.."

"Your wife." Roman finished.

"My wife. I gotta win her back."

"I hear you. Me and Erica figured this would be an option, so let's make this happen. I called a few guys. Tomorrow we'll put some work on tape and send it. Show them you, we still got it."

"Aiight, bet that." Shawne replied.

The following day, several college and pro players, including Big Bo, met Shawne and Roman at the USC practice facility'

"Y'all not doin' this without me. This reunion ain't complete without me!" Bo said with excitement.

"Beef, you're still under contract for another year." Shawne tried to exclaim.

"And you're my agent. Make it happen."

"You heard the man. Make it happen!" Roman laughed.

They got out on the field and executed plays and routes almost to perfection. There was no rust. Shawne looked like a kid again.

Jackson contacted scouts and general managers with not only LA, but several other teams. He knew the more interests Shawne and Roman could draw, the better chance of getting exactly what they wanted. All in attendance were very impressed with the performance. That night, Jackson called Shawne with news.

"We got offers. Oakland and Frisco both offering a three year with a team option fourth year twenty mil. New York is offering a three year twenty-two million, fully guaranteed. And LA is offering 2 years, seventeen million, but full of incentives and bonuses."

"And Roman?" Shawne inquires.

"The same. New York is the better option."

"Naw. This ain't about money. Counter LA's offer with this." Shawne writes down his counter offer. "If they agree, it's on."

Jackson looked at it. "Are you sure?"

"Trust me." Shawne nodded.

Shawne discussed the offer with Roman and Erica. They were good with it. The next morning, Jackson called Shawne. "They like it. Working on it as we speak. You want me to set a press conference for this afternoon?"

"Let's do it tomorrow. I wanna break the news to the fam first." Shawne answered.

Shawne first called Travis. He told him his decision on returning to the league, and that he was dedicated to his craft. He also thanked him for not only taking him under his wing back at Lincoln, but becoming his spiritual big brother. Travis guided Shawne through some of the darkest days of his life. He also asked if Travis would remarry him and Jazmin if they were to get back together. Travis said it would be his honor.

He texted Tiffany and asked her to come over. While he waited for her, he texted Kimistry.

'Hey Miss Lady. I hope all is well for you. Just wanted you to know, next season I'll be back on the field, well, maybe the sidelines. News breaks tomorrow. I'll be playing here in LA. Maybe you should have taken the job. Free massages! LOL! Just Jokin'. Just wanted you to know. Keep takin care of yourself. XOXO'

There was a knock at the door. "Come on." Shawne said.

Tiffany opened the door.

"Hey Tiff." He greeted getting up to hug her.

"What's up?"

"I'm getting back in."

"And?" She asked after he stopped abruptly.

"And I'm staying right here. I wanted you to know before the news conference tomorrow. And I want you to know I heard you. Years ago, and months ago. That you want your little brother in your life the way we were growin' up. I remember that time you gave me one of your chains to give to Jaz as a gift. You've always had my back. I know it feels like I turned my back on you as I got older. I'm sorry it feels like that, but that was never my intention. I love you Sis! Always." Shawne extended a closed hand out to her. She reached back to accept. He placed keys in her hand.

"What's this?" She asked.

"This loft is yours now. I know you've been rentin' an apartment since you left your husband. This is much bigger, and much cheaper."

"And where do you plan on stayin'?"

"Lord willing, I can go home. If not though, Lil Shawne will have to live here with you, and I'll stay at the office when I'm in town." He joked.

Tiffany was speechless. She and Shawne were so much alike. Never willing to show weakness or that she needed help. She was very grateful to Shawne.

"I don't know what to say or how to repay you." She said in a shy tone.

"Just say '*Thank you Lil Bro. I love you.*' And repay me with a hug."

Tiffany grabbed a hold of Shawne, kissed on his cheek, and hugged him.

"I wouldn't trade you for a million dollars. Thank you. I love you so much!"

She held onto him for what seemed like an eternity.

After Tiffany left, Shawne and Ta' Shawne fell asleep. He was awakened by a knock at the door. It was Jazmin and KayKay.

"Hey. Come on in. I'm glad you're here. I wanna talk to y'all." Shawne said, stretching and rubbing his eyes as they sat down.

"Daddy, let me go first please. I'm sorry for getting mad at you and being selfish. I know how much you love to play football..."

"No no no no, CoCo-Pop. Stop right there. You have nothin' to be sorry for. I should have put you and Mommy first a long time ago. Yes, I do love football, but not at the cost of losing you." He looks at Jazmin.

"So you're not going back?" Jazmin asked.

"Actually I am. Announcing it tomorrow."

"Where? What's the terms?"

"Yeah, where?" Kayla asked.

"I'm stayin' right here. Roman will sign a two year twenty million dollar contract. I took a two year twelve million dollar fully guaranteed. And they traded their backup QB and a 2nd round draft pick to New York for Bo. Then, they'll sign their new franchise Left Tackle to a four year thirty million dollar contract. But of course, you will have to look it all over first." Shawne said with a huge smile.

"You sound like an agent that has it all figured out." Jazmin complemented.

Just then, Ta'Shawne came out of the room, yawning and wiping his eyes. He climbed onto Jazmin's lap and rested his head on her shoulder and wrapped his arms around her neck. She instantly melted, smiling from ear to ear.

"Aww Mommy, Shawny loves you! And Daddy is staying home!" She yells and jumps onto his lap.

Jazmin looks at Shawne and the kids, and emotions overtake her.

"Baby, take you brother into the other room. Let me and Daddy talk." Jazmin told Kayla.

"Okay Mommy. Come on Shawny."

As Jazmin set Ta'Shawne down to the floor, he kissed her on the cheek.

"I love you Mommy." He said and followed his big sister into the room.

Jazmin closed her eyes, tearing up uncontrollably.

"Shawne, you've made mistakes, and I've made mistakes, and still… The love has never faded. In fact, I love you more now than I may ever have. Everything about us, all the faults, all the wrongs, completes us as one."

"What are you sayin' Jaz?" Shawne asked

"I'm saying I want us to be an us again. You. Me. And our two beautiful children. Yes, both our children. Before you ask or question, I fell in love with that precious little boy the day I met him. Your son is my son. He's our son. "Are you ready to make this union whole again?" She extends her closed hand out to him.

"And Arthur? Or Stephon, whatever his name is. What about him?" Shawne asked.

Jazmin shook her head.

"That's long over with. It's just me and you. I promise." Jaz assured.

Shawne took her hand.

Before he would accept whatever is in her hand to give him, knelt down on a knee.

"Jazzy Baby, I wanna start fresh. I wanna earn your love. I wanna court you again, take you out. With and without the kids. Baby, this time,

I will love you as Christ loved the Church. Will you do me the honor of remarrying me?"

With free hand, she caressed his face, crying and nodding her head as she answered '*yes*'.

She handed him the keys to the house. "Come home." She commanded.

"I'm glad you said that!" Shawne laughed.

"Why? What happened?"

" I just gave this loft to Tiffany." They both laughed. KayKay and Lil Shawne run into the living room.

"What's so funny?" Kayla asked.

"We are. Come here." Shawne said to her. He hugged Kayla tightly, and kissed her forehead as Jazmin hugged and squeezed Ta'Shawne. Shawne was overwhelmed with gratitude and joy. He begins to choke on tears, looking upwards thinking how proud Tasha, Coach Brown, his parents and little sister must be in heaven smiling down at him right now, as he gave thanks to his Lord and Savior for keeping him, and his family.

The next day, Shawne made his announcement. He signed, Roman signed, Bo was traded, and he signed his four year deal as planned.

Shawne entered the season as QB2, but in the first quarter of the first game, LA's All-Pro starting quarterback tore his ACL and was done for the season. Shawne entered the game and remained the starter for the remainder of the season going 11-5 and making it to the conference championship before losing a heartbreaking 23-21 on a missed field goal.

Roman had a great season, but it was overshadowed by the birth of his son, Roman Cali Goodman. Erica insisted on their son being a junior, but Roman wanted to honor his brother.

Crystal continued to stand by her man, even working on an appeal for him. Derek remained positive and optimistic through his renewed faith. He and Shawne still met weekly and he was still very much a part of building Day One Sports into a conglomerate.

Shawne's relationships with his aunt and mother in law got stronger being back home. He saw his own mother in both of them and loved them both dearly for always treating him as their own.

Shawne spoiled all the kids. Kayla, Lil Shawne, DJ, Tiffany's kids and was waiting for Baby Cali to get older to join in. Movies, weekend camping trips, sleepovers. They did it all. Shawne and Tiffany's relationship was back on track as well. They talked daily, and hung out from time to time.

Jazmin's love for Ta'Shawne was undeniable. If you didn't know it, you would think he was birthed by her. She loved that boy and he loved her. He'd cry when she dropped him off to school and nothing or no one else seemed to matter to him when she was around.

Shawne kept his promise. In the offseason, Travis came out to LA and officiated the renewal of their vows. As a second honeymoon, they sailed the Pacific Ocean for a week on a yacht. An all inclusive for two, with a full time chef and butler.

Shortly after returning home, Jazmin began craving pizza with yogurt and throwing up in the morning. Uh-oh Shawne, Number three?

The End

Printed in the USA
CPSIA information can be obtained
at www.ICGtesting.com
LVHW040741131023
760664LV00002B/309

9 798888 104309